PUFFIN CLASSICS
The Final Adventures of Professor Shonku

The Final Adventures of Professor Shonku

SATYAJIT RAY

TRANSLATED FROM THE BENGALI BY SATYAJIT RAY
AND INDRANI MAJUMDAR

Introduction by DHRITIMAN CHATERJI

PUFFIN BOOKS
An imprint of Penguin Random House

PUFFIN BOOKS

USA | Canada | UK | Ireland | Australia
New Zealand | India | South Africa | China

Puffin Books is part of the Penguin Random House group of companies whose
addresses can be found at global.penguinrandomhouse.com

Published by Penguin Random House India Pvt. Ltd
4th Floor, Capital Tower 1, MG Road,
Gurugram 122 002, Haryana, India

First published in Puffin Books by Penguin Random House India 2020

Text and Illustration copyright © The Legal Heirs of Satyajit Ray 2020
This translation copyright © Indrani Majumdar 2020
Introduction copyright © Dhritiman Chaterji 2020

Pages 252–253 are an extension of the copyright page.

ISBN 9780143447023

Typeset in Minion Pro by Manipal Technologies Limited, Manipal
Printed at Replika Press Pvt. Ltd, India

www.penguin.co.in

Contents

Introduction

Professor Enigmatic

It's been about three months since Sandip Ray's *Professor Shanku O El Dorado* released in theatres. It was a film in the making for a while, given the demands of special effects and other logistics, and that necessitated living with the character for an extended period—definitely longer than what I am normally used to. One of the interesting rediscoveries I made about the character while preparing to play him is how difficult to fathom Shonku is. As I see it, that's probably because the Shonku stories are chronicles from his diaries discovered after he disappears. This is unlike, say, the Feluda stories in which young Topshe gives us heaps of information on the sleuth.

No one has ever met Shonku in flesh and blood, so to speak. There is no 'real' Shonku to go back to and ask questions. He comes across as enigmatic. The language and tone of the stories, as it should be in a diary, is very even-handed, there's very little emotion or drama in the writing, though the events being described are very dramatic. One has to try and read between the lines to get to the core of the character.

In the first couple of stories in the Shonku canon, Satyajit Ray depicted him as the typical eccentric, somewhat irritable genius one is used to imagining. From the early sketches, it is clear he was cast very much in Conan Doyle's Professor Challenger mode. However, Ray quickly changed that characterization and Shonku became a serious, reputed scientist, as comfortable in his little provincial laboratory in Giridih as in international forums. Challenger himself, by the way, was based on two people Doyle knew, a psychologist and a medical doctor.

In one story, Shonku describes himself as what amounts to saintly, peaceful and patient. That became the Shonku persona. It is only towards the end, in one of the last stories, that you get a sort of flesh-and-blood picture of the man as Shonku reminiscences and talks about his father and his values. You get an inkling of the old-world values that shaped him, deduce what might have made him choose to stay back in Girdih whereas a genius like him should actually have found far greener pastures.

The stories, as we all know, started appearing in *Sandesh* magazine in 1961—and in fact they came about as part of Ray's efforts to revive *Sandesh*. The first collected volume was published in 1965 and was dedicated to his son Sandip. Ray always loved a play on words and it is not surprising that he dedicated it to Sandip 'Babu'—Babu being Sandip's nickname. I was well past college by this time, so can't claim truthfully that I grew up reading Shonku! It was courtesy the film project that I read more Shonku than I probably would have otherwise.

Normally, I am not a great believer in a lot of analysis, a lot of workshopping, etc., in playing a character. Instinct plays a great part in what I do. I try and follow the director's vision and the screenplay, which is my Bible. If I haven't read the original text, I normally don't read it once I get the screenplay, so as to avoid confusion. With Shonku, things were a little different. I had to try and dig deeper. That's primarily because the stories are written in diary form. From the diary where he's describing events, places and so on, I do not get a great deal of insight into his personal character other than his physical characteristics, which I get from Satyajit Ray's sketches.

Later on, thinking about it, I realized that part of what writers, film-makers and other creative people personally are reflects in the characters that they create. Satyajit Ray was a cosmopolitan man, a citizen of the world. At the same time, he was 100 per cent Bengali. If you think about it, Shonku too is like that. He keeps to himself, his experiments, his work. At the same time, when he goes on his many adventures and to international conferences, he is equally at home. There are two sides to the character.

I suspect the difficulty in getting a feel of the character extends to translating Shonku too. And that is where I feel Indrani Majumdar has done a terrific job. I have read Shonku in the original fairly widely. As far as reading him in translation goes, I have read Indrani's translated volume *The Mystery of Munroe Island*. In fact, just the other day I was reading a particular story side by side with the translation. It struck me again how intelligent her rendering is. If you are unaware of the Bangla, you could read the English as original and not be able to tell that it comes from another language, which quite an achievement. Ray's Bangla writing, particularly for children, is not only lucid and descriptive, it is also very pictorial. You can see the events unfolding, as they say, in front of your eyes. At the same time, his style is not quite what we call *chalti* bhasha or colloquial language. It is literary. And it is never easy to communicate the flavour of that in a translation. Definitely not with Shonku, where you have to be alive to the fact that the target audience is the child and the young adult.

In one of the stories, for example, Shonku is talking about how he sees himself and how the world sees him. A section of the scientific community considers him a charlatan. Ray uses the word 'pretoshiddho'. Now, I claim to know my Bangla reasonably well but that isn't a word I have come across, and definitely not in a story meant for children. Indrani translates the word to 'witch doctor', which isn't a literal translation but it conveys the sense of the original wonderfully. I found that commendable. And that is true of the stories in this collection too. I am inclined to not call them translations, but very faithful renderings which keep intact the sequence, flow and chronology, but most importantly the nuance of the original. We often tend to rate translations one rung lower than originals in the hierarchy of literary works. Reading these translations one realizes how unfair that can be. The best of translators strive to make the translation an original.

I can probably say with some surety that I have not come across a mind as varied as that of Satyajit Ray. The range of subjects he was interested in was legion. Of course, it is as a film-maker that he is known internationally, and rightly so. However, his achievements span an incredible range: typography, illustration, music, writing. He had what I can describe as an active, curious mind. I have personally discussed the high arts of philosophy, anthropology, philology with him. At the same time, he was extremely interested in crime fiction. I have been a lover of crime fiction for the longest time, but even I was not aware of the pulp detective fiction he introduced me to. He was also hugely interested in riddles, puzzles, stories about little-known but fascinating places. All of that shows in his writing for children. Though he was a relatively well-travelled man, given the many film festivals he had to go to, the places he brings to life in his pages, in Shonku as well as the Feluda stories—Mexico, China, the Pacific, the Amazon, the European continent during the Second World War—are in many ways journeys of the mind.

It's been as rewarding reading these translations as it was getting to play the character in the film. In Feluda and Shonku, we have the finest writing for children anywhere in the world. And why just children, grown-ups are avid readers too. It is always interesting to compare these two characters, as I am sure many of you do. Both of them are part of the same milieu as Ray himself: well-spoken, articulate, the quintessential educated middle-class bhadralok. What's also fascinating to dwell upon is the absence of any women in their lives. Does that owe itself to a puritanical streak in the author? That's another subject for Ray enthusiasts to ponder and debate.

Dhritiman Chaterji
March 2020
Goa

1

Tellus

12 March, Osaka

There was a demonstration of Tellus today in the presence of more than three hundred scientists and a hundred journalists from all over the world. Tellus was placed on a three-foot-high pedestal of transparent pellucidite on the stage of the hall of the Namura Technological Institute. When two of the workers of the institute came in carrying the smooth, elegant platinum sphere, the hall echoed with spontaneous applause. That an apparatus which can answer a million questions should be only as large as a football, weigh forty-two kilos and bear no resemblance to a machine, came as a complete surprise to the audience. The fact is, in this age of microminiaturization, no instrument, however complicated, need be very large. Fifty years ago, in the age of cabinet radios, could anyone have imagined that one would one day be watching television programmes on one's wristwatch?

There is no doubt that Tellus is a triumph of modern technology. But it is also true that in the making of intricate instruments, man comes nowhere near nature yet. The machine we have constructed contains ten million circuits. The human brain is one-fourth the size of Tellus, and contains about one hundred million neurons. This alone indicates how intricate is its construction.

Let me make it clear that our computer is incapable of mathematical calculations. Its job is to answer questions which would normally require a person to consult an encyclopaedia. Another unique feature of the computer is that it gives its answers orally in English, in a clear, bell-like tone. The first question has to be preceded with the words 'Tell us', which activate the instrument and which gives it its name. At the end the words 'Thank you' turn it off. The battery, whose life is one hundred and twenty hours is of a special kind, and is housed in a chamber inside the sphere. There are two hundred minute holes on the surface of the sphere covering an area of one square inch; these allow the questions to enter and the answers to come out. The questions have to be of a nature which calls for short answers. For instance, although the delegates were briefed before today's demonstration, a journalist from the Philippines asked the instrument to talk about ancient Chinese civilization. Naturally, no answer came out. And yet when the same journalist asked about certain specific aspects of specific Chinese civilizations, the instrument astonished everyone by answering instantly and precisely.

Tellus can not only supply information, but is also capable of reasoning logically. The biologist Doctor Solomon from Nigeria asked the instrument whether it would be safer to keep a young baboon before a hungry deer or a hungry chimpanzee. Tellus answered in a flash! 'A hungry deer'. 'Why?' asked Doctor Solomon. Came the answer in a sharp, ringing voice: 'Because the chimpanzee is carnivorous.' This is a fact which has only recently come to light; even ten years ago everyone thought that monkeys and apes of all species were vegetarian.

Besides these, Tellus is able to take part in games of bridge and chess, point out a false note or a false beat in music, identify ragas, name a painter from a verbal description of one of his paintings, prescribe medicines and diets for particular kinds of ailments, and even indicate the chances of survival from the description of a patient's condition.

What Tellus lacks are abilities to think and feel, and supernatural powers. When Professor Maxwell of Sydney University asked it if a man would still be reading books a hundred years from now, Tellus was silent because prognostication is beyond it. In spite of these deficiencies, Tellus surpasses human beings in one respect: the information fed into its brain suffers no decay. The most brilliant of men often suffer from a loss of faculties with age. Even I, only the other day in Giridih, found myself addressing my servant Prahlad as Prayag. This is the kind of mistake which Tellus will never make. So, in a way, although it is a creation of human beings, it is more dependable than man.

The original idea for the instrument came from the famous Japanese scientist Matsue, one of the great names in electronics. The Japanese government approved of his scheme and agreed to bear the expenses of constructing it. The technicians of the Namura Institute put in seven years of hard labour to construct Tellus. In the fourth year, just before the preliminary work was over, Matsue invited seven scientists from five continents to help feed information into the computer. Needless to say, I was one of the seven. The other six were Doctor John Kensley of Britain, Doctor Stephen Merrivale of the Massachusetts Institute of Technology, Doctor Stassof of the USSR, Professor Stratton of Melbourne, Doctor Ugati of West Africa and Professor Kuttna of Hungary. Of these, Merrivale died of a heart attack three days before leaving for Japan. He was replaced by Professor Marcus Wingfield from the same MIT. Some of these scientists have stayed the full stretch of three years as guests of the Japanese government. Others, such as myself, have come for short stretches at regular intervals. I have been here eleven times in the last three years.

I should like to mention an extraordinary event. The day before yesterday, on 10 March, there was a solar eclipse.

Japan fell in the zone of totality. Because it was a special day, we had already decided to finish our work before the tenth. We thought we had done so on 8 March when we discovered that no speech was coming out of the machine. The sphere was built so that it could be taken apart down the middle. We did that. Now we had to find out which of the ten million circuits was at fault.

We searched for two days and two nights. On the tenth, just as the eclipse was about to begin—at 1.37 in the afternoon—a high-pitched whistle issued from Tellus' speaker. This indicated that the fault had been repaired. We heaved a sigh of relief and went out to watch the eclipse. I wondered if there was any significance in the fact that the beginning of the eclipse coincided exactly with the coming to life of the instrument.

Tellus has been kept at the institute. A special room has been built for it to keep it under controlled temperature. The room is a most elegant one. Tellus rests on the concave surface of the pellucidite pedestal in the middle of one side of the room against the wall. On the ceiling is a hole through which a concealed light sends a powerful beam to illuminate the sphere. The light is kept on all the time. Because Tellus is a national treasure, the room is guarded by watchmen. One must not forget that even nations can be jealous of one another; I have already heard Wingfield grumble twice about the USA losing the race to Japan in computer technology. A word about

Wingfield here. There is no question that he is a qualified man; but nobody likes him very much. One probable reason is that Wingfield is among the most glum-faced of individuals. Nobody in Osaka remembers seeing him laugh in the last three years.

Three of the scientists from abroad are going back home today. Those who are staying behind are Wingfield, Kensley, Kuttna and myself. Wingfield suffers from gout and is getting himself treated by a specialist in Osaka. I hope to travel around a bit. I'm going to Kyoto with Kensley tomorrow. A physicist by profession, Kensley's interests range wide. He is something of an authority on Japanese art. He is most anxious to go to Kyoto if only to see the Buddhist temples and the Zen gardens. The Hungarian biologist, Krzystoff Kuttna, does not much care for art, but there is one thing that interests him which only I know of, because I am the only person he discusses it with. The subject does not come strictly under the province of science. An example will make it clear.

We were having breakfast together this morning. Kuttna took a sip of coffee and said quite unexpectedly, 'I didn't watch the eclipse the other day.'

I wasn't aware of this. For me the total solar eclipse is a phenomenon of such outstanding importance. The corona around the sun at the time of totality is for me such an extraordinary sight that I never notice who else is watching besides me. I was amazed that Kuttna could deprive himself of such an opportunity. I said, 'Do you have any superstition about watching an eclipse?'

Instead of answering, Kuttna put a question to me: 'Does a solar eclipse exert any influence on platinum?'

'Not that I know of,' I said. 'Why do you ask?'

'Why then did the sphere lose its lustre during those two-and-a-half minutes of totality? I clearly noticed a pall descending on the sphere as soon as totality began. It lifted the moment totality ended.'

I didn't know what to say. 'What do you think?' I asked at last, wondering how old Kuttna was and whether this was a symptom of senility.

'I have no thoughts,' he said, 'because the experience is completely new to me. All I can say is that if it turns out to be an optical illusion, I would be happy. I am not superstitious about an eclipse, but I am about mechanical brains. When Matsue asked me to come, I told him about it. I said, if man continues to use machines to serve human functions, there may come a time when machines will take over.'

The discussion couldn't go on because of the arrival of Kensley and Wingfield. What Kuttna felt about machines was nothing new. That man may one day be dominated by machines has been a possibility for quite some time. As a simple example, consider man's dependence on vehicles. Even city dwellers, before the days of mechanical transport, used to walk seven or eight miles a day with ease, now they feel helpless without transport. But this doesn't mean that one should call a halt to scientific progress. Machines *will* be made to lighten the work of man. There is no going back to primitive times.

14 March, Kyoto

Whatever I have read or heard in praise of Kyoto is no exaggeration. I wouldn't have believed that the aesthetic sense of a people could permeate a whole city in such a way. This afternoon we had been to see a famous Zen temple and the garden adjoining it. It is hard to imagine a more peaceful atmosphere. We met the famous scholar Tanaka in the temple. A saintly character, his placidity harmonizes perfectly with his surroundings. When he heard about our computer, he smiled gently and said, 'Can your machine tell us whose will works behind the sun and the moon coinciding so perfectly for a solar eclipse?'

A true philosopher's question. The moon is so much smaller than the sun, and yet its distance from the earth is such that it appears to be exactly the same size as the sun. I had realized the magnitude of the coincidence as a small boy. Ever since then I have had a feeling of profound wonder at the phenomenon of total eclipse. How can Tellus know the answer to the question when we don't know it ourselves?

We will spend another day here and then go to Kamakura. I have benefited a lot from Kensley's company. Good things seem even better when you are with someone who appreciates them.

15 March

I am writing this in the compartment of our train in the Kyoto station. There was a severe earthquake here last night at 2.30 a.m. Tremors are common in Japan, but this one was of a great magnitude and lasted for nine seconds. But this is not the only reason we are returning. The earthquake has precipitated an incident that calls for our immediate return to Osaka. Matsue phoned at five this morning and gave me the news.

Tellus has disappeared.

It wasn't possible to talk at length over the telephone. Matsue speaks in broken English anyway. In his agitation, he could barely make himself understood. This much he told us: Immediately after the earthquake, the pellucidite pedestal was seen lying on the floor and Tellus was missing. Both the guards were found lying unconscious and both had had their legs broken. They are in the hospital now, and haven't yet regained consciousness. So it is not yet known what brought them to this state.

In Kyoto, ninety people were killed by houses collapsing. In the station, everybody is talking of the earthquake. To be honest, when the tremor started last night, I too felt helpless and uneasy. I had run out of the hotel along with Kensley, and we could make out from the vast crowd outside that everybody had come out.

What a calamity! So much money, labour and experience had gone into the making of the world's most sophisticated apparatus, and in three days it disappears.

15 March, Osaka, 11 p.m.

I am sitting in my room in the International Guest House which faces the Namura Institute across a public park. From the window could be seen the tower of the institute. It is no longer there; it came down during yesterday's earthquake.

Matsue came to the station with his car to receive us. The car took us straight to the institute. One of the guards has regained consciousness. His story goes like this: His friend and he had both considered running out into the open when the earthquake started, but hearing a sound from Tellus' room they had unlocked the door and gone in to investigate.

The guard's version of what happened thereafter is wholly unbelievable. What they saw upon entering the room was that the pedestal was lying on the floor while Tellus was rolling from one end of the room to the other. By then the tremor had abated in intensity. Both the guards had advanced towards the sphere to capture it. At this, the sphere had come charging towards them and hit them in their legs with force enough to break their bones and render them unconscious.

If the story of the ball rolling by itself is not true, the other possibility is theft. That both the guards were a little drunk has been admitted by Konoye, the one who has regained consciousness. In that state, it was not unnatural that they would both dash out of the building; there were people working in the laboratory that night, and everybody had run out into the compound. This means that most of the doors were open. There was nothing to prevent outsiders from entering the institute. A clever thief could easily have taken advantage of the panic and made off with a forty-two-kilogram sphere without anybody noticing.

Theft or no theft, Tellus was no longer in its place. Who has taken it, where it is at the moment, whether there is any possibility of retrieving it are questions which remain unanswered. The government has already announced that whoever finds Tellus will get a reward of 500,000 yen. The police have started their investigations. Meanwhile, the second guard has regained consciousness and vehemently asserts that the sphere was not stolen but, guided by some mysterious force, had assaulted its protectors and made its escape.

Only Kuttna believes the guards' story, although he is unable to support it by any rational explanation. Kensley and Wingfield both believe that theft is the only possible explanation. Platinum is a most precious metal. These days the younger generation of Japanese are quite capable of doing reckless things under the influence of drugs. Some of the more radical amongst them would be quite prepared to undertake such a robbery if only to embarrass the government. If such a group has made off with Tellus, they will surely extract a high price before giving it up.

The search will not be easy, for the agitation over the earthquake hasn't subsided yet. More than a hundred and fifty people have been killed in Osaka, while the number of those injured exceeds two thousand. And there is no guarantee that there will be no more tremors.

Kuttna was here till a little while ago. Although he believes that Tellus escaped on its own, he cannot find a reason for it doing so. He believes that crashing on the floor during the tremor has done something to its innards. In other words, Tellus has lost its mind.

I myself feel wholly at a loss. This is an unprecedented experience for me.

16 March, 11.30 p.m.

Let me set down the nerve-racking experiences of today.

Of the four of us, only Kuttna is able to hold his head high because his guess has turned out to be largely correct. I doubt if anyone will have the temerity to work on artificial intelligence after this.

Last night, after I had finished writing my diary, I found it difficult to go to sleep. Finally, I decided to take one of my Somnolin pills. As I left my bed to get the phial, my eye was drawn to the north window. This is the window that looks out over the park and faces the Namura Institute. What caught my eye was the light from a torch in the park. The torch was being turned off and on and roved over a fairly large area.

This went on for about fifteen minutes. It was clear that the owner of the torch was searching for something. Whether he succeeded or not I do not know, but I saw him picking out his way with the help of the torch as he finally left the park.

This morning I described the incident to my three colleagues. We decided to take a look in the park after breakfast.

At about eight, the four of us set off. Like most other cities of Japan, Osaka is not flat, and one has to climb up a slope before reaching the park. The path in the park winds through flowering trees and bushes. Maple, birch, oak and chestnut abound. The Japanese had started a long time ago to uproot their own trees and plant English ones instead.

After walking for about fifteen minutes, we met our first stranger: a Japanese schoolboy, about ten years old, with pink cheeks, close-cropped hair, and his satchel around his shoulder. The boy halted in his tracks, and was now looking at us with an expression of alarm. Kuttna knew Japanese. 'What is your name?' he asked the boy.

'Seiji.'

'What are you doing here?'

'I'm going to school.'

'What were you looking for in the bush?'

The boy said nothing.

Meanwhile, Kensley had moved over to the right. 'Come here, Shonku,' he called out.

Kensley was looking down at the grass. Wingfield and I joined him and found that a patch of grass and a sprig of wild flower had been flattened by something rolling over them. A few feet away we saw a flattened lizard.

This time the boy had to answer. He said he had seen a metal ball behind a bush on his way back from school yesterday. As he had approached it, the ball had rolled away. He had kept chasing the ball for a long time but had failed to catch it. Coming back home he had heard on the television about the reward. So, he had looked for the ball with a torch the night before but had not found it.

We told the boy that if we found the ball in the park, we would see that he got his prize. The boy looked relieved, left his address and ran off to school. The four of us split up and went off in four directions to look for the sphere. Anybody finding it would call out to the others.

I left the beaten track and started looking behind bushes. If Tellus had really become mobile, it was doubtful whether it would surrender. On top of that, if it has developed an antipathy to human beings, it would be hard to predict what it might do.

Casting wary looks around, I walked for another five minutes when I found a couple of butterflies lying on the grass. One of them was dead, while the other's wings still flapped weakly. It was clear that something heavy had passed over them only a little while ago.

I now proceeded slowly and with great caution when I was pulled up short by a sudden sharp sound. If one were to describe it in words, it would be—'Coo-ee!'

I was trying to locate the source of the sound when I heard it again—'Coo-ee!'

This was unmistakably Tellus, and the sound could only mean one thing: It was playing hide-and-seek with us.

I didn't have to go far. Tellus was behind a geranium tree, glistening in the sunlight. It didn't move at my approach.

It must have been the 'Coo-ee' that had told the others of Tellus' proximity. All three converged on the same spot. The smooth metal sphere made a strange contrast with the surrounding vegetation. Was there a slight change in Tellus' appearance? That we can tell only if we removed the dust and grass from the surface.

'Tell us—tell us—tell us . . . '

Kensley knelt on the grass and called out the two words to activate Tellus. We were all anxious to find out if it still functioned.

'In which battles was Napoleon victorious?'

The question came from Wingfield. The same question had been asked by one of the journalists on the day of the demonstration, and Tellus had answered instantly.

But no answer came today. We exchanged glances. My heart filled with a deep foreboding. Wingfield moved up closer to the sphere and repeated the question.

'Tell us what battles Napoleon won.'

This time there was an answer. No, not an answer, but a counter-question. 'Don't you know?'

Wingfield was flabbergasted. Kuttna's mouth had fallen open. The fear mixed with his look of surprise was characteristic of someone confronted by a supernatural event.

Whatever the cause, Tellus was no longer the same. By some unknown means, it had surpassed the skill human beings had endowed it with. I was sure that one could converse with it now. I asked it:

'Did someone bring you here or did you come by yourself?'

'I came by myself.'

Kuttna put the next question. He was excited to the point where his hands trembled and beads of perspiration showed on his forehead.

'Why did you come?'

The answer came like a flash.

'To play.'

'To play?' I asked in great surprise.

Wingfield and Kensley were now squatting on the grass. 'A child must play,' said Tellus.

What kind of talk was this? The four of us now spoke almost in unison.

'A child? You are a child?'

'I am a child because you are all children.'

I don't know how the others felt, but I could see what Tellus was trying to say. Even towards the end of the twentieth century, man has to admit that what he knows is very little compared with what he doesn't. Gravity, which pervades the universe and whose presence we feel every moment of our existence, is to this day a mystery to us; we are indeed children if we take such things into account.

The question now was: what to do with Tellus. Now that it had a mind of its own, it would be best to ask it. I said, 'Have you finished playing?'

'Yes, I am growing older.'

'What will you do now?'

'Think.'

'Will you stay here, or come with us?'

'Go with you.'

'Thank you.'

We picked up Tellus and started on our way back.

On reaching the guest house, we sent for Matsue. We explained to him that it wouldn't do to keep Tellus in the institute any longer because one would have to keep an eye on him all the time. At the same time, it wouldn't be wise to make any public statement about his present state.

In the end, it was Matsue who decided on the course of action. There were two trial spheres made before the one that was actually used. One of them would be kept in the institute and an announcement made to the effect that the sphere had been retrieved. The real Tellus could be kept in the guest house where there were no other residents apart from the four of us. It was a two-storey building with sixteen rooms. The four of us were occupying four rooms on the first floor. We could communicate with each other by phone.

Within a few hours, a glass case arrived in my room from Matsue. Tellus has been placed in it in a bed of cotton. While wiping the dust from the sphere I noticed that its surface was not as smooth as before. Platinum is a metal of great hardness, so that in spite of all the rolling the sphere had done, there was no reason for it to lose its smoothness. In the end, I asked Tellus. After a few moments' pause it answered:

'I do not know. I am thinking.'

In the afternoon, Matsue arrived with a tape recorder. The speciality of this particular model is that it starts recording the moment a sound is produced, and stops as the sound stops. The recorder has been kept in front of Tellus. It'll work by itself.

Matsue is overcome by a feeling of helplessness. All his mastery over electronics is of no use in the present situation. He wanted to take apart the sphere and examine the circuit but I dissuaded him. I said, 'Whatever may have gone wrong inside it is important that we shouldn't interfere with what is happening now. Man is able to build a machine, and will do so in future too, but no human skill can produce an object like Tellus as it is now. So all we do now is keep observing it and communicating with it.'

In the evening, the four of us were sitting in our room having coffee when we heard a sound from the glass cage. A well-known, high-pitched, flutey sound. And yet nobody had said the two words to switch it on. Tellus was obviously able to activate itself. I went over to the cage and asked: 'Did you say anything?'

The reply came: 'I know now. It is age.' Tellus had found the answer to the question I had asked in the morning. The roughness of the sphere was a sign of ageing.

'Are you old now?' I asked.

'No,' said Tellus. 'I am in my youth.'

Among the four of us, only Wingfield's behaviour seems a little odd to me. When Matsue suggested taking Tellus apart, it was only Wingfield who supported him. He regrets that Tellus is no longer serving the purpose for which it was built. Whenever Tellus starts to talk on its own, Wingfield appears to feel ill at ease. I agree Tellus' behaviour has something of the supernatural about it, but why should a scientist react like that? In fact, today it gave rise to a most unpleasant incident. Within a minute of Tellus' talking to me, Wingfield left his chair, strode up to the glass cage and said, 'What battles did Napoleon win?'

The answer came like a whiplash.

'To want to know what you already know is a sign of an imbecile.'

I can't describe the effect the answer had on Wingfield. The words that came out of his mouth were of a nature one would scarcely associate with an aged scientist. Yet the fault was Wingfield's. That he could not accept Tellus' transformation was only an indication of his stubbornness.

The most extraordinary thing, however, was Tellus' reaction to Wingfield's boorishness. 'Wingfield, I warn you!' I heard it say in a clear voice.

It was not possible for Wingfield to stay in the room any longer. He strode out, shutting the door behind him with a bang.

Kensley and Kuttna stayed on for quite a while. Kensley feels Wingfield is a psychopathic case who shouldn't have come to Japan. As a matter of fact, Wingfield has made the least contribution among the seven of us. Had Merrivale been alive, things might have been different.

We had dinner in my room. None of us spoke, nor did Tellus. All of us noticed that the sphere was getting rougher by the hour.

After my two colleagues left, I shut the door and sat down on the bed. Just then, Tellus' voice set the tape recorder in motion again. I moved up to the glass cage. Tellus' voice was no longer high-pitched; a new solemnity had come into it.

'Are you going to sleep?' asked Tellus.

'Why do you ask?'

'Do you dream?' came the second question.

'I do sometimes. All human beings do.'

'Why sleep? Why dream?'

Difficult questions to answer. I said, 'The reasons are not clear yet. There is a theory about sleep. Primitive man used to hunt for food all day and then sit in the darkness of his cave and fall asleep. Daylight would wake him up. Perhaps we still retain that primal habit.'

'And dreaming?'

'I don't know. Nobody knows.'

'I know.'

'Do you?'

'I know more. I know how memory works. I know the mystery of gravity. I know when man first appeared on earth. I know about the birth of the universe.'

I was watching Tellus tensely. The recorder was turning. Was Tellus about to explain all the mysteries of science?

No, not so.

After a pause, Tellus said, 'Man has found the answer to many questions. These too he will find. It will take time. There is no easy way.'

Then, after another pause: 'But one thing man will never know. I too do not know it yet, but I will. I am not a man; I am a machine.'

'What are you talking about?'

But Tellus was silent. The recorder had stopped. After about a minute it turned again, only to record one word: 'Goodnight'.

18 March

I am writing my diary in the hospital. I feel much better now. They will release me this afternoon. I had no idea such an experience awaited me. I realize what a mistake I had made in not taking Tellus' advice.

The day before yesterday, I went straight to bed after saying goodnight to Tellus. I fell asleep within a few minutes. Normally I sleep very lightly and wake up at every sound. So when the phone rang I was up at once. The time on my travelling clock with the luminous dial was 2.33 a.m.

It was Wingfield calling.

'Shonku, I've run out of sleeping pills. Can you help me?'

I said I'd be over in a minute with the pill. Wingfield said he would come himself.

I had brought out the phial from my suitcase when the doorbell rang. Almost at once came the voice from the glass cage: 'Don't open the door.'

I was startled. 'Why not?' I asked.

'Wingfield is evil.'

'What kind of talk is that, Tellus?'

The doorbell rang again, and was followed by Wingfield's anxious voice.

'Have you fallen asleep, Shonku? I've come for the sleeping pills.'

Tellus had given its warning and fallen silent.

I was in a dilemma. How could I not open the door? How could I explain my action? What if Tellus' warning was baseless?

I opened the door. Something descended with force on my head and I lost consciousness.

When I came to, I was in a hospital. Three scientists stood at my bedside—Kensley, Kuttna and Matsue. They provided me with the details.

Having knocked me out, Wingfield had taken Tellus apart and taken the hemispheres into his room. He had put them in his suitcase, waited until dawn, and then gone down and asked the manager to arrange a car for him to take him to the airport. Meanwhile, the porter who had brought Wingfield's luggage down had been suspicious about the great weight of the suitcase, and had informed the policeman on duty at the gate. The policeman had challenged Wingfield, and the latter had desperately pulled out his revolver. But he wasn't quick enough. He was now in custody. It is suspected that he may be responsible for his colleague Merrivale's death in Massachusetts. He was afraid that Tellus, with his supernatural abilities, would reveal unpleasant facts about him. This is why he was anxious to run away with the sphere, hoping to dispose of it somewhere on the way to the airport.

'Where is Tellus now?' I asked after I had listened to the extraordinary story.

'It is back in the institute,' replied Matsue. 'You see, it was no longer safe to keep it in the guest house. It is back in his place on the pedestal. I put it together again.'

'Has it said anything since?'

'It has asked to see you,' said Matsue.

I couldn't contain myself any more. To hell with the pain in my head—I had to go to the institute.

'Can you make it?' asked Kuttna.

'I'm sure I can.'

Within half an hour, we were in the elegant room once again. Tellus was seated on its throne on the pedestal, bathed in the shaft of light from the ceiling. I could see there were cracks all over the sphere. There was no question that these four days have aged Tellus considerably.

I went over and stood near it. Before I said anything, I heard its calm, grave voice.

'You have come at the right time. There will be an earthquake in three-and-a-half minutes. A mild tremor. You will feel it, but it will do no damage. As the tremor ends, I will know the answer to my last question.'

There was nothing to do except wait with bated breath. A few feet above Tellus was the electric clock whose second hand moved steadily along.

One minute . . . two minutes . . . three minutes . . . We watched with amazement at a glow beginning to pervade Tellus as the cracks widened. The colour of the sphere was changing. Yes, it was turning into gold!

Fifteen seconds . . . twenty seconds . . . twenty-five seconds.

Just at the stroke of the half hour, the floor under our feet shook, and in that very instant, the sphere exploded into a thousand bits and scattered on the floor. Then, from the ruins was heard an eerie, disembodied voice declaiming—

I know what comes after death!

Translated by Satyajit Ray

2

Professor Rondi's Time Machine

7 November

It's rare that three scientists in three different parts of the world are all conducting research on similar equipment at the very same time. However, that's exactly what has been going on of late. I happen to be among these three scientists and the gadget I am working on is a time machine.

Ever since my days as a student, when I'd read H.G. Wells's amazing book, *The Time Machine*, I've nursed this great aspiration to invent such a machine myself. The desire is no longer confined to wishful thinking alone. I've put in some real hard work already. It is no longer confined to only a hypothesis or to my imagination. The theory gathered steam when I read out my paper on this subject in a science meet in Madrid last February. The presentation earned me a lot of praise. Yet, due to insufficient funds and the non-availability of the right tools and gadgets, my work in this area could not proceed any further.

In the meantime, I learned from my old German friend Wilhelm Crole that Professor Kleiber of the city of Cologne in Germany has been working on a time machine as well, and making good progress. Kleiber had attended my lecture in Madrid and that's when I met him. Unfortunately, before he could complete his work, he lost his life in the hands of an unknown assailant. This had occurred a fortnight ago. Physicist Kleiber was a wealthy scientist; he had many interests in addition to this area of science. One such passion was collecting valuable artefacts. The murderer could have been a burglar as three valuable art objects had gone missing from Kleiber's study, the room where he was murdered. Kleiber had been bludgeoned to death with a blunt object. Despite a thorough search, the police are yet to locate the weapon and the assailant too still remains at large.

The third person working on a time machine at present is a Milan-based Italian physicist, Professor Louise Rondi. Rondi's machine is complete and it has had a round of demonstrations as well. Rondi wasn't present in Madrid and I'd no knowledge of his involvement in this area of research. After reading his handwritten letter a month ago, I came to know that his time machine was now ready. He has warmly invited all of us to visit Milan to examine his machine. I am aware of my strong apprehension that I'd lose out in this competition but it is beyond me to predict how he has actually achieved his goal. I'm thinking of taking a trip to Milan this month. Rondi's not just taking care of my hospitality; he has offered to pay for my air travel too. In fact, Rondi is an extremely well-to-do man. He is known not just as a professor; he is, in fact, Count Louise Rondi. Therefore, it's easy to infer that he owns huge assets. However, in this present context I can understand his feelings. After all, it requires a true scientist to value and appreciate such a significant discovery. Since I haven't been successful in this experiment yet, Rondi can't quite relax till he displays his machine to me. Spending an amount to the tune of Rs 20,000–30,000 is nothing for an affluent scientist like him.

I must describe the time machine to those who have no knowledge of what it is. With the help of this machine, one can travel either to the past or to the future. There's still a difference of opinion among scientists on how the pyramids of Egypt were built. With the help of a time machine a person can now travel 5000 years back in time and can personally observe how these imposing structures were constructed. Why just 5000 years, one can travel, say, 7.5 million years back simply to see what kind of creature the dinosaur was. Does this journey imply that you need to travel physically, in person? I cannot quite comment on this till I see Rondi's machine. It could be that your body remains static, but what unfolds before your eyes are the images of old times just like a movie. Not bad! What more can you ask for? If mankind today can watch prehistoric cavemen or witness the wars involving Alexander and Napoleon or even see what this world will look like 20,000 years hence, what an extraordinary achievement that would be!

I've decided I shall accept Rondi's invite. Like a child, I'm extremely curious about this machine. I can't possibly let go of an opportunity to see it.

12 November

Yet another letter from Rondi. While I've already replied to his previous letter, he must have written me this one before he received my reply. Clearly, he is waiting to receive a eulogy from an internationally acclaimed scientist with much eagerness. Today, I sent off a telegram mentioning the date and time of my arrival.

Meanwhile, trouble came knocking at my door.

Out of the blue, Nakurbabu made an appearance. I've mentioned him earlier. A very gentle and unassuming man. In fact, he can be too callow and virtuous, yet on occasions he seems to possess such uncanny and supernatural powers that he is able to perceive things beyond the capacity of any normal person. One of his extraordinary faculties is his ability to read the future—it is as if this gentleman turns himself into a live time machine.

Like he does always, Nakurbabu touched my feet and apologized for disturbing me. Then, sitting down on the sofa, he began speaking, warning me that I might have to face some danger in the distant future. His visit was meant to caution me.

I asked, 'Danger? What sort of?'

Clasping his hands, he said, 'Well, I can't describe your risk precisely but I can sense a serious peril awaiting you, one that might even endanger your life. Hence, I thought I ought to inform you.'

'Will I survive this danger?'

'That I can't tell, sir.'

'Can you tell me when this is likely to strike?'

'Yes, sir, that I can,' Nakurbabu answered with conviction. 'The incident will take place on 21 November at 9 p.m. I cannot say anything more, sir.'

I'll be reaching Milan on the 18 November. One can see that this predicted incident will come about while I'm there. As far as I know, Rondi is a noble-hearted man. I've never heard of anything malicious about him. Will the danger in that case emerge from Rondi's machine?

Whatever the case, I have to face the circumstances. It won't be such a bad idea to travel to the past as well as to the future, at least once, before I die!

18 November, Milan

I arrived here this morning. Humming with activity, this ever-busy, modern-day metropolis is one of the noted business centres of Italy. Rondi lives in his castle, a little beyond the outskirts of the city, in a somewhat secluded area. Rondi himself came to the airport to fetch me. Courtesy his refined and polished appearance, it's impossible to guess that he is only fifty-two years old. Not a single strand of white hair is visible; even his French beard and moustache are jet black.

On our way from the airport, Rondi removed his clay pipe from his mouth and said, 'Even though I did not attend your lecture, I read it in our paper *Il Tempo* as they had reproduced your talk. How unfortunate that you could not create the machine.'

What Rondi said next left me completely baffled.

'In my letter I did not disclose the real reason for my invite to you. I shall tell you now. My machine is working rather well. It can travel to and fro to the future as well as to the past. If you know the exact geographical location of a particular place you want to visit, you can easily reach that very spot. For instance, yesterday I visited Greece prior to the BC era and for a brief spell witnessed a debate amongst the Greek philosophers. This was in the afternoon. However, if I wanted to reach there early in the morning or at some other specified time I couldn't have done so as I am yet to decipher the technique to organize such time synchronization on my own machine. I've failed in this regard. If you help me with this, I'll offer you a partnership in my company.'

'Company?' I asked, surprised.

'Yes, company,' said Rondi, a faint smile on his lips. 'It's called Times Travel Incorporated. Whoever puts in money will be able to travel in the future or the past according to their choice. I'd placed only one advertisement in a New York paper. Within a period of three weeks I've received three-and-a-half thousand enquiries. Of course I'm not going to launch my company before January but I can well predict that business will be booming.'

'How much money does it require to undertake this journey?'

'That would depend on the distance, time and the period of the journey—to the future or the past. The rate for visiting the future will be more expensive than that for the past. As for the past, in order to visit a historical age, the rate is ten thousand dollars for ten minutes. If it's prehistoric, the rate will be double. Also if the trip requires more than the stipulated ten minutes, the rate will increase to thousand dollars per minute.'

'What about the future?'

'For the journey to the future there's no difference in rates. Whether you want to travel to the near future or to the distant future the rate has been fixed at 25,000 dollars per trip.'

I couldn't help but appreciate his business acumen. I realized in no time that this upstart's business will be a rollicking success, all thanks to these countless dollars.

I posed a more important question.

'What exactly is the role of a visitor in your time machine? Will he be able to physically mark his presence in the future or in the past?'

Rondi shook his head.

'No, definitely not physically. The visitor will be present not in person but in an invisible state. No one can see him. Yet he will see everything. Depending on which part of the world one chooses to visit, the machine will be preset to the longitude and latitude of the place. There are different buttons to determine which period of the past and the future one chooses to visit. After you press these various buttons, it'll take about ten seconds to reach the specific age and place. Once you reach the spot, the rest will be a cakewalk. Suppose you have arrived in Cairo via this machine and from there you want to visit the pyramids of Giza, you can do that instantly. In other words, the locations may change according to the traveller's plans as long as the period remains the same.

'Which means you arrive in the past or the future location of your initial choice but then from there you can take off to any other destination?'

'Yes, but as I've mentioned, my machine has no hold over the exact time of the day or night for any trip. Yesterday, I had pressed the button to visit Altamira of 30,000 BC— to observe how the prehistoric artists had painted on the walls. However, I arrived on a new moon night and thus I could see almost nothing in the darkness. Maintaining the same period, I changed the location and opted for Mongolia where dawn had just broken. But this didn't quite serve my purpose either. Hence it's my request that you examine my machine.'

I said, 'That's precisely why I've come here. However, I can't promise you anything right now regarding improving your machine. Also many thanks for offering me partnership in your company; but there's no need for it. I'll be grateful if my work alone proves my personal scientific merit.'

Rondi gave me a peculiar smile as if to say what a strange man I was. I had so easily turned down such a grand chance to earn a great deal of money.

It was around 12 noon when I finally reached Rondi's residence. Rondi himself took me to my room. The arrangements were excellent. There will certainly be no negligence in his hospitality.

When I asked Rondi if he lived alone in this palatial house, he answered that he had a modern apartment in Rome where his wife and daughter live. 'Once every two months I go to Rome to spend a week with them. As this is a much bigger house it helps me to work better,' Rondi explained. 'My laboratory and equipment are all here and my assistant Enrico too stays with me. Moreover, at present I have many scientists from all over the world coming to visit me to look at my machine. They come for a day and stay overnight. I've had thirty such visitors and they have all wholeheartedly acknowledged my success.'

It was decided that I'd study his machine after lunch and only then would I come to a decision about Rondi's request. The time machine I had worked on could reach the exact time and date of travels both in the future as well as the past. Even if my machine were similar to Rondi's in all respects, I still can't say whether I would be able to accomplish what he wants me to.

Now I must stop writing and head for a bath. Rondi has already informed me that lunch will be served at 1 p.m.

18 November, 4 p.m.

I'm in no position to describe my present state of mind.

Today, I travelled to the kingdom of Emperor Ashoka and visited his veterinary hospital all thanks to Rondi's machine. It's not that the visuals are crystal-clear. It's somewhat like looking through a mosquito net. Yet, it's so very thrilling, I was almost choked with excitement. We have all read in history that Ashoka had enforced a law to stop the killing of animals and had also established a veterinary hospital to cure injured and ailing animals but had I ever envisaged that I would actually witness such a hospital? What I saw were hundreds of cows, horses, goats and dogs under one roof, all being treated at once! I could also hear the noise of people at the hospital talking to each other. It sounded like the filtered noise heard through earplugs. These sounds reached me almost in whispers. I am not sure whether this was the limitation of the machine, or it was simply not possible to see or hear anything clearer than this. I can only check this when I examine the machine. Today, my role was chiefly that of a traveller. Tomorrow, I have to scrutinize the machine thoroughly. All I can say at this point is that there's a lot of similarity between the machine of my imagination and that of Rondi's. Therefore, I feel I may perhaps be able to help Rondi.

The machine is placed in the middle of a medium-sized room, occupying almost all of it. It stands on a platform about two feet in height and is enclosed within a transparent chamber with a door fixed in the middle. The traveller needs to stand in the middle of this chamber. All the details have to be given to Rondi beforehand, so that when the passenger enters the chamber, Rondi can press all the relevant buttons for the traveller to embark on the journey. Individuals can control the logistics of the journey from inside the cubicle though Rondi has decided to control even this himself. The return from the future or the past is preset. Anyone travelling for, say, ten minutes needs to make use of that entire time unless someone else presses a button to bring that person back.

After entering the chamber, when the traveller presses the button he will experience a mild electric shock. At that instant, a black screen will unfold before him. After a few seconds, a new scene will appear on the screen. I saw myself, at forenoon, standing in front of a wide royal pathway lined on both sides with pillars. Pedestrians, bullock carts and occasional horse-drawn chariots were moving about. On the two sides of the roads were finely carved two-storeyed wooden houses, all in very pleasant surroundings. As I was more interested in the emperor's veterinary hospital my wish altered the scenario and I found myself inside the hospital.

I had no idea how the time flew. When Rondi pushed the button at the end of the stipulated ten minutes, I felt an electric shock once more and with it everything darkened and moments later I found myself back in the machine room. When Rondi asked for my reaction, I congratulated him warmly on his invention and promised to do my best to attend to his request.

Today, I met Rondi's assistant, Enrico. He is about thirty, handsome and intelligent. I can't fathom exactly why but I thought I detected a touch of distress on his face. I know it's not easy to judge a man in such a short time. After talking to Enrico, I realized that he knows a lot about India. He said his grandfather was an Indologist and was well versed in Sanskrit. This made me quite curious.

I asked him, 'What's your surname?'

Enrico said, 'Petri.'

'Does that mean you're Ricardo Petri's grandson?'

Enrico nodded. I've read quite a few books on India written by Petri. Naturally, I felt an affinity with Enrico. Given a chance, I'd love to speak more to him.

Tomorrow morning I'd like to begin my work on the machine. Rondi said he will arrange for more assistants, if need be.

19 November

As a representative of India and of science, I've done my country very proud. With only Enrico's help, and working for just three hours I've added such a dimension to Rondi's machine that it can now accomplish all of Rondi's requirements. Two-and-a-half thousand years ago in Babylon where Nebuchadnezzar ruled, streets dazzled with petroleum lights. After pressing a button on the time machine, I arrived in Babylon at 8.30 p.m. in order to view this sight. I don't think I can describe an experience like this in a few simple words. All I felt was that historians will now no longer need to depend on their imagination in order to describe the past. Now on, they will see everything with their own eyes and then start documenting. Though I doubt if any historian will be able to afford Rondi's steep rates! I've discussed this with him and realized that he is not at all thinking of historians or researchers. All he wants is to make utmost profit through this machine. Therein lies a massive gap between his ethos and mine. I wonder how this jolly fellow can actually be such a shark. All the same, one must admit that he is a very gifted scientist as well as an inventor. There is no doubt that he will be remembered as an immortal character in the world of science.

Today Rondi advised me to spend a few more days here and also to gather some more exposure to time travel through his machine and then return home. I've no objection to that. Time travel can become such an addiction; and there's no dearth of places to visit. Tomorrow, I'd like to go and look into the future. Those who write science fiction have imagined the future in very many ways. I would love to see if their conjectures match up to the reality. Will humankind really turn out to be such willing slaves to machines? I certainly believe so.

19 November, 11 p.m.

My Munich-based German friend Wilhelm Crole called me this evening. I'd informed him in my letter that I'm staying at Rondi's house in Milan. Crole jokingly remarked that one fellow working with the time machine had already been murdered; we should make sure that we don't meet with the same fate.

Crole also mentioned that that there had been no breakthroughs yet in Kleiber's murder. Kleiber's research in this machine project was more advanced than mine. Had he been alive for another month, his machine would have been completed.

Ever since dinner I have been feeling rather uncomfortable. My head feels heavy and is reeling at times; the rest of the body too feels fatigued and exhausted. I always carry with me my wonder drug pill Miracurall, which cures all ailments. So far I've never had to take it. Today I shall take one. It's pointless to fall ill abroad.

20 November, 1 p.m.

A strange incident took place today. Don't tell me Nakurbabu's predictions will turn out to be true! To start with my pill has worked. I feel better today. I noticed the improvements after I woke this morning. The fatigue is no longer there. Yet to be safe all I consumed at breakfast was some toast and coffee. When Rondi commented on this I told him about my indisposition and also informed him about my wonder pill. Rondi heard this with great attention. When I glanced at Enrico, I noticed a deep crease on his forehead and a look of restlessness.

Rondi asked, 'Which century would you like to travel today?'

I said, 'A millennium in the future.'

'To which country?'

'Japan. Because I feel Japan will outshine other countries in future technology. Hence the impact of scientific progress will be best captured in Japan.'

Rondi said he needed to go out in the morning. He'd open the machine room after he returned at 11 a.m.

I ought to mention one thing here. The room in which the machine is kept remains locked round the clock and the key rests only with Rondi. So, unless and until Rondi opens the door there's absolutely no way you can reach the machine. Yesterday, while I worked on the machine Rondi remained with me all the time. Each time I went inside the machine, Rondi stood next to me and pressed all the required buttons. There's no doubt that Rondi is extremely possessive about his machine. Yet there's a provision of a burglar's alarm. The main door is always bolted. Even if the windows remain open there are armed guards keeping a vigil on the outside. Is Rondi trying to protect the machine particularly from me or does he doubt Enrico as well?

After Rondi left, I went to the library to collect some scientific journals and then returned to my room. After half an hour, there was a knock on the door and I found Enrico, standing in front of me, looking pale.

I invited him to come inside and asked, 'What is it?'

'Danger,' Enrico said in a heavy voice.

'Who is in danger'?

'You. And if it gets known that I've warned you, I am too.'

'What danger are you talking about?'

'I'm convinced that there was poison mixed in your fruit juice last evening.'

This unexpected information left me speechless for a while. Then, I enquired, 'What makes you think so?'

'That's because we too consumed the same things except the fruit juice. It was meant just for you. And it was only you who fell ill.'

'But why?'

'I think he will not accept any kind of competition as he fears this will jeopardize his business. He wants to be the sole proprietor. Let me narrate an incident that will clarify this matter. The day he completed his machine, in sheer happiness, he drank too much. I happened to come across him in this drunken state without his knowledge. I would rather not repeat the words he used to swear at both his rivals, Kleiber and you. By then Kleiber, of course, had already lost his life but in his inebriated state Rondi kept cursing you. He is convinced that you will get in the way. You've no real idea about this man. Only when he is intoxicated can you see his actual self. You've already noticed the way he is shielding his machine. He is allowing you to use the machine only because he plans to eliminate you soon. Rondi has never allowed anyone from the scientific fraternity visiting him to use the machine more than once. I'm his assistant. For three years I have been working beside him; yet when the machine was completed he never even allowed me to touch it.

I was surprised to hear this. 'You still haven't travelled on it?'

'I've taken a trip,' said Enrico, 'but without the professor's knowledge. Last month he had gone to Rome. During that time, just like a robber, I opened the bolt of the machine with a wire. Following this same procedure, I continue to enjoy such trips every night. I'm now addicted to it. Though I've no idea what will befall me if by chance the professor gets to know of this.'

'Do you suggest that I get away from this place?'

'If you stay back, make sure you don't consume any item which we're not having. It's not difficult for him to finish you off by adding poison to your food.'

I remembered Nakurbabu's warning. I said, 'My own medicine will protect me from all poison.'

'But if he gets to know this secret he'll opt for some other means.'

'But I won't give him any such option. I'll pretend that my medicine is no longer working on me. I can do that. In any case I thank you immensely for alerting me.'

Enrico left. I sat on the bed plunged into deep thought. Suddenly something occurred to me and I decided to call up my friend Crole. Within a minute we were connected.

'What's up, Shonku? Is anything the matter?'

I narrated to Crole about what had happened to me. After listening to me, Crole asked, 'This lad Enrico . . . is he prone to an excitable imagination, would you say?'

I said, 'No. I believe what Enrico told me. I know I can handle this present situation. I'm calling you now not to take your help in this matter but to seek some information.'

'What information?'

'First things first. Tell me, has Kleiber's murderer been arrested?'

'Why do you ask?'

'I've my reasons.'

'Yet to be caught but the weapon has been located . . . concealed under his garden. But no fingerprints were found. Hence the mystery remains.'

'On which date was he murdered?'

'Let's see . . . 23 October. Would you also like to know the exact time?'

'Yes, it may help.'

'What exactly are you planning on?'

'Oh, nothing, just my indomitable curiosity.'

'In that case let me tell you . . . a journalist had come to meet Kleiber at 7.30 p.m. The visitor left after half an hour. Soon after, Kleiber's retainer discovered his dead body.

According to the forensic report the murder took place between 7 and 8 p.m.'

'Many thanks.'

'Please take care and don't involve yourself in any misadventure unnecessarily. Why don't you swing by Munich?'

'If I remain alive!'

After placing the receiver down, I became immersed in thought.

It's 9.45 a.m. Rondi had said he would return by 11 a.m. A plan came to my mind. It will help me immensely if I can accomplish it in the meantime. However, I can't carry this out on my own. I need Enrico's help. Enrico lives on the first floor. I know his room.

I went straight down to his room. He was inside. 'You need to open the machine room. I ought to take a trip. Right now.'

He swung into action. Enrico's skill with the wire was amazing. Almost like the use of a real key the door opened swiftly. I needed Enrico to be with me. Suppose there was some trouble while I'm on my journey he could bring me back to the present.

'Will you be travelling to the future or the past?' asked Enrico.

'To the past. To be precise, 23 October, 7.25 p.m. I'm establishing the exact location using the geographic map. While looking at a huge map hanging on the wall I dictated the precise longitude and latitude of Cologne to Enrico. Enrico pressed the button soon after I had entered the machine.

After covering a cross section of the city of Cologne, as planned, I reached Kleiber's house. It's best I waited there. The journalist should appear within five minutes. There was still some hint of an evening light. Kleiber's house, a neat two-storeyed building, faced a garden. I could hear a female voice from inside the house calling out someone's name. Kleiber was a little over forty. I'd read in the paper that he died leaving behind his wife and two children.

After five minutes I heard the sound of car. A Mercedes taxi stopped in front of the house. A man of medium height stepped out. He was bearded and wore a long overcoat over his dark blue suit. He also sported a hat and carried a briefcase. After paying the driver, the visitor walked up to the front door and pressed the calling bell. Almost immediately, a servant opened the door.

'Is the professor in?' asked the stranger. He then took out a card from his pocket and, handing it over, said, 'I made an appointment over the phone.'

Even though the stranger tried to alter his voice, it somehow sounded familiar to me.

The servant took the card inside and returned almost immediately. He asked the visitor to come in. I followed suit.

The visitor took off his overcoat, handed it over to the retainer, placed his hat on the hat stand and glanced at

47

himself in the mirror. Following the retainer's instruction, he entered a room through a rear door and so did I. It was indeed thrilling to know that I could observe everything while I remained invisible.

The room was Kleiber's study, his workspace. Kleiber sat behind a large table in a leather-bound chair. He stood up and shook hands with the stranger. Kleiber was tall, decorous, blonde, with a thin gold moustache and wore a golden pair of glasses. Kleiber pointed towards a chair opposite his table. I stood in front of the closed door. It seemed as if there was a thin screen in front of me and through that I saw the stranger taking out a packet of cigarettes from his pocket and offering one to Kleiber. When Kleiber refused the visitor himself put a cigarette in his mouth and, picking up the silver lighter from Kleiber's table, lit his cigarette and put the packet back in his pocket. This followed a series of questions and answers related to Kleiber's time machine. I was devoid of any feeling of heat or cold, yet watching the way both of them were rubbing their hands I could see they were feeling the chill. There was a lit fireplace on one side of the room. Kleiber got up to go towards it to adjust the fire, his back facing the stranger. Taking full advantage of Kleiber bending down to get the fire going, the stranger took out a blunt iron rod from inside his coat sleeve and struck it on Kleiber's head. Kleiber's lifeless body dropped down on the floor. The stranger picked up three small statues that stood on a mantelpiece and placed them inside his briefcase.

Right at this moment the sound of footsteps outside the door alerted the stranger. He turned rather pale. But the sound soon faded. Seizing the moment the stranger left the room, the weapon once more concealed inside the sleeve of his coat.

I followed the stranger.

Outside, the retainer reappeared bearing the overcoat. After putting it on, the stranger proceeded towards the main door.

It's now pitch-black outside. Despite this, the stranger buried the rod in one corner of the garden and proceeded towards the gate. At this precise moment, I realized my journey had come to a halt.

'I can hear the professor's car,' said Enrico in a measured tone.

Both of us stepped out of the machine room. Once more with the help of the iron wire Enrico locked the room skilfully. The sound of a car door opening and closing reached us from outside. Within a minute, I was back in my room.

Now I know the killer of Kleiber is none other than Rondi himself. But what's the point of this knowledge? How can I prove it? Especially, because a long period of time had passed since the incident. Even after thinking hard, I could arrive at no solution.

I must go down now. Rondi's retainer, Carlo, has informed me that his boss was waiting for me in the machine room.

22 November

I returned to my country today. That I could come back safely is a matter of great fortune that can be explained only after I describe in detail the sequence of events that followed. Due to the last two days of excitement, tension and indisposition, there was no way I could attend to my diary.

That day after receiving Rondi's order, I went down with much reluctance. Rondi's instinct was very sharp and he could sense my uneasiness. When he questioned me about this, I had to take refuge in deception.

I said, 'As my medicines didn't work properly I feel rather weak.'

I may be wrong but I clearly noticed Rondi's eyes sparkling. He said, 'Why don't you try one of my Italian medicines?'

Simply not to provoke any further suspicion, I said, 'Well, I don't really mind giving it a try.'

Of course, I knew too well that if I had to take a medicine with water, Rondi would definitely add poison to the water. But if I continued to have Miracurall, no poison could ever harm me. Also, I knew that Rondi couldn't commit a murder in Enrico's presence. He would opt for a course that would entail a slow death for me. Let him persist with his acts while I continued to feign illness just to convince him that his scheme was indeed working.

On the ground of my illness, the plan of a visit on the time machine got postponed. Rondi brought me the medicine. A pill, naturally. After taking it along with the water, also brought by Rondi, and allowing a gap of half an hour I took Miracurall.

But for how long can I go along with this farce? Since I finally had with me a real clue of Rondi as Kleiber's murderer, I couldn't possibly leave for my country without making sure that Rondi faced punishment.

Yet I can't seem to think of any way out.

During lunch, Rondi enquired how I was feeling. I replied, 'I think I feel some strength returning but I'll eat very little.'

At this point, I exchanged a glance with Enrico who was sitting right next to me. With great dexterity, he pushed a chit of paper into my right hand during our meal. After finishing lunch, when I returned to my room, I read the chit which said, 'I would like to meet you this afternoon.'

Enrico arrived around 2.30 p.m. He said, 'Since the professor's sudden arrival, I have had no chance to find out about the result of your visit to Cologne.'

I said, 'What if the professor comes to know of your visit here?'

Enrico said, 'It's the professor's age-old habit to sleep at least for an hour in the afternoon. I'm sure you know of our Italian custom of the siesta—people of this country love to take a break in the afternoon.'

After giving an explicit description of my trip, I told Enrico, 'There's no doubt left that Professor Rondi is the culprit behind Kleiber's killing. Though he was in disguise I could identify him by his voice. The problem is how do we prove him to be guilty? Where's the proof?'

Enrico said, 'Professor Rondi didn't actually go to Rome when he had said so. I found this out from a friend of mine in Rome. One can then infer that he had actually gone to Cologne. But I don't think this can be treated as evidence at all.'

I shook my head. 'Just because you didn't go to Rome doesn't in any way prove that you took a trip to Cologne.'

At this point, I couldn't help but disclose certain information to Enrico.

'A psychic friend of mine has predicted that a great danger awaits me at 9.30 p.m. on 21 November. But he couldn't foresee if I would outlive the danger. I'm keen to know how exactly this danger will hit me.'

'Are you thinking of taking the help of the time machine?'

'Yes.'

'In that case let's move fast,' Enrico proposed. 'We still have thirty-five minutes before the professor wakes up. We can't afford to delay any further.'

We made our way to the machine room. Enrico said, 'I can't give you more than ten minutes.'

I said, 'That will do.'

I stood inside the plastic cage. This time I personally pressed all the buttons. After ten seconds I saw myself standing in front of the famous Milan cathedral. The scene I witnessed left me astonished.

After this, with the help of my willpower, when I entered my own room in Rondi's castle, I saw myself, i.e., Trilokeshwar Shonku, lying still in my own bed. In a second, I gathered I was seriously ill. All my belongings were strewn across the room as if someone had rummaged through my stuff in great haste, though I couldn't comprehend why.

Even though I took pity on the state I saw myself in, I could do nothing. I kept tossing and turning in my bed restlessly; once, I got up and struck my head, and lay down immediately in a state of remorse. I seemed to be cracking up in an act of intense regret.

Suddenly there was a knock at the door. The figure on the bed glanced at the door and at that instant Rondi entered. Watching his ruthless appearance my blood curdled.

'In today's dinner I deliberately mixed an extra dose of poison in your water,' declared Rondi, 'so that you'll never be able to raise your head again. Well, if you continue to live and if you build your own time machine it will create a hurdle in my business and that's something I cannot allow. I want you to rest your body peacefully in Milan. Many people are dying here due to some unknown viral infections about which the doctors have no clue. You too will die under similar circumstances. Within twenty-four hours . . .'

The scene ended abruptly, bringing down the black screen.

I found myself back inside the machine room.

'Sorry, Professor,' said Enrico. 'Ten minutes are over. We ought to run now.'

In spite of not knowing whether I'd survive this threat, an idea struck me right then. It was so exciting that my hands started shaking.

'What's the matter, Prof. Shonku?' asked Enrico.

I somehow controlled myself and answered, 'An idea has come to my mind. We need to complete two errands. One is to call up my friend in Munich.'

'And the second?'

'It's you who need to attend to this task. It calls for courage and I know you have the strength.'

'What work?'

'I have noticed a huge collection of pipes in Rondi's study. At least twenty to twenty-two pipes are on display. You need to take one of them and give it to the police to test for his fingerprints. Can you?'

'That's easy,' said Enrico. 'I'm acquainted with the police force here. It was I who organized the police post for this house.'

'Well, then that takes care of that.'

We left for our respective rooms. Enrico promised me that by evening he would manage to obtain a pipe and immediately try to reach the police station.

After returning to my room, I made a call to Crole and informed him of the necessary matter. I desperately needed his help . . . without it my mission couldn't be accomplished. Crole too assured me that there would be no failing from his side.

All this took place day before yesterday, i.e., on 20 November.

The next day, on 21 November, nothing remarkable happened. However, I ought to mention one incident. Rondi has been enquiring about my health constantly. I think that he is feeding me poison and I too am consuming my Miracurall to ward off the reaction, keeping my body hale and hearty, yet pretending to be weak. Keeping this scenario in mind I did wonder if Rondi was seeing through my act but the man was far too clever to let in on what was going on in his mind. Yesterday, post lunch, I finally came face to face with his cunning.

After lunch, when I returned to my room and reached out for Miracurall, I realized that the bottle was not where it should have been—inside my handbag. It was missing. I was stricken with fear. Shivers ran down my spine. It's doomsday if I couldn't counter-attack the effect of the poison.

Like a lunatic I ran helter-skelter looking for my medicine though I was positive it could only have been inside the bag. Eventually, feeling utterly helpless, I called Enrico but he too was not in his room. I could feel my

body turning numb. Rondi may have increased the dose of poison so that within a few days, I'd be done with.

Left with no choice I lay down. A horrible pain was spreading over my entire body. My limbs were growing numb and my head was reeling. I had no idea when I had fallen asleep in such a state. When I woke up it was late in the evening.

I rang up Enrico once more. He still hadn't returned to his room.

I could no longer stand up straight and so went back to bed. My vision was slightly blurred. Had my last moments already arrived? I noticed the time on the travelling clock placed on the table. It said 9 p.m. This means . . .

Yes, I had indeed seen this on my time machine. After knocking at my door, Rondi entered my room and began to threaten me. I had already heard this yesterday; but I was to hear it once more.

'Many people are dying here due to some unknown viral infections about which the doctors have no clue. You too will die under similar circumstances. Within twenty-four hours everything will be over, I believe. After this Louise Rondi will become the sole proprietor of the time machine. There's no dearth of money in my life, yet the greed for it can be such an incurable addiction . . .'

Knock . . . knock . . . knock . . .

Rondi trembled in fear. He had locked the room from inside.

Knock . . . knock . . . knock . . .

Rondi remained seated. His face had turned white; his eyes were wide open.

Gathering all my power, I got up from my bed. Stumbling, I somehow pushed Rondi aside to open the door and then collapsed on the ground, senseless.

Armed police entered the room.

Both Crole and Enrico had stood by me like genuine friends. The day I'd entered Kleiber's room via the time machine I'd seen Rondi lighting his cigarette using Kleiber's lighter. Perhaps he had planned to take it with him but in haste had forgotten to do so. Despite having seen this, it had clearly not registered on my mind. When finally everything dawned upon me I immediately called Crole to inform him that the murderer's fingerprints could be found on the lighter and they would definitely match with the fingerprints on Rondi's pipe.

That's exactly how everything worked out.

My Miracurall bottle was found in Rondi's room. After consuming a pill, it took me only four hours to get back to my normal healthy self.

3

Nefrudet's Tomb

7 December

I have just received a telegram from my German friend, Crole. He writes:

> Drop all your work at once and come over to Cairo. Another mausoleum has been discovered on the likes of Tutankhamen's tomb. The tomb is situated two miles from the southern part of Saqqara. I'm arranging a room for you at the Karnak Hotel in Cairo.
>
> —Wilhelm Crole

We all know that when any king or a high official died in ancient Egypt, their bodies were embalmed into what are known as mummies and then placed inside coffins or a sarcophagus and finally stored inside an underground room. The ancient Egyptians believed that a person's life doesn't come to an end even with death, and hence the need to use everyday objects doesn't cease. Therefore, food, toys, cosmetics, jewellery, furniture, and clothes—all found their place within the tomb. Among these, some items were indeed very valuable like stone and inlaid gold ornaments. Once, even a throne made of solid gold was found in one such tomb. The coffin that encased the mummy of Tutankhamen was made of pure gold. Nowhere in the world could one come across such a large amount of pure gold all at once.

Due to the presence of such precious objects, robbers have since ancient times looted the crypts. With the result that, at present, very few tombs are left with any valuable objects. The sole exception is Tutankhamen's tomb. This young emperor's tomb has, surprisingly, been spared. In 1922, Howard Carter's discovery of the tomb created a worldwide stir primarily because nothing was missing from the crypt.

I have read about the tomb Crole mentions. This happens to be a 3500-year-old tomb belonging to one priest-cum-magician called Nefrudet. After obtaining permission from the Egyptian government, Lord Cavendish of England has decided to support the entire cost of this tomb's excavation. Even though the work is being carried out by people of different countries, the Egyptian government has laid down a condition: a part of whatever is found will go to the government. That's how such amazing museums have come up in Cairo. This excavation work of Nefrudet's tomb is being supervised by the young archaeologist, Joseph Bannister. A newspaper reported on this recently dug room and judging by the report it appears that no robber has yet assaulted this tomb. I'd read about this three days ago. By now, the work must have progressed further, though work of this nature can be very time-consuming. To me this is a god-sent opportunity. Crole is a much-respected name within the fraternity of archaeologists. As he is now an intrinsic part of this project I too will face no difficulty in joining this group.

It's not that Lord Cavendish has a particular fondness for Egypt. He has many other interests too. He is the owner of huge assets in England. At various times and in various places he has sponsored many ventures out of which the Brazil and New Guinea expeditions come to mind.

All I know about Joseph Bannister is that he is thirty-five years of age and an authority on Egypt.

I'll be leaving in three days. I've always nursed a tremendous curiosity about Egypt. At my ripe old age, I'm brimming with excitement like a young boy.

12 December, Cairo

It's now 11.30 p.m. I'm writing my diary sitting in room number 352 of Karnak Hotel. I arrived in Cairo yesterday morning. Crole was present at the airport. On our way from the airport to the city, I got all the news of the last three days. There's no doubt left that this tomb has remained untouched by invaders, primarily because the entry point of the crypt was concealed under a few boulders. Joseph Bannister knew of Nefrudet and was convinced that his tomb must lie hidden somewhere. When he was about to give up after many attempts, as a last try, he asked for these stones to be removed. Within moments, it became obvious that there was something definite underneath. After further digging, it became apparent that this was indeed an entry point. Bannister was sure that this particular spot was the main gate of the tomb as the threshold bore the name of Nefrudet written in an ancient Egyptian script.

Soon after this discovery, Bannister telephoned Lord Cavendish in London. Cavendish asked him to continue with the excavation and assured him that there would be no dearth of funds.

Yesterday afternoon I visited the spot with Crole. I was introduced to Bannister. A very intelligent and enthusiastic fellow, he is all agog with excitement about his work. He is convinced that he is about to embark on a discovery similar to that of Tutankhamen, though the former was a king and the latter a priest and magician.

The first room excavated revealed numerous items, the majority of which were idols of gods and goddesses and

some furniture. The workmanship was of a superior quality. After each item in the first chamber had been numbered and photographed with utmost care, these were being sent to a laboratory for a clean-up.

Crole has organized himself well. He has known Bannister for quite some time. After speaking with Bannister, he has obtained permission for us to be present inside the chamber where the digging is taking place.

In the meantime, reporters from across the world have started arriving here. Of course, they're not allowed on the dig and will not be allowed to enter the main door. They are gathering whatever information they can get only from the outside.

At the back of the first chamber lies a sealed door. There's no doubt that this will lead to another room. Who knows what stuff is concealed there!

15 December

Today the second room was opened. Bannister went inside carrying a torch and looked at the room for a while, alone. Crole and I waited outside. When eventually these rooms get electric connection, we won't need to depend on a torch. Soon, we were called in. In an animated voice Bannister said, 'This room too has many objects. The number of caskets alone is eleven, in various sizes. And caskets would obviously suggest that each of these will be full of stuff.'

I've seen the caskets of the Tutankhamen tomb. Those boxes were made of ivory, wood and alabaster, with exquisite inlay work done on the body of them. The boxes in this tomb are similar. Apart from this, one also notices a few things which were not present in Tutankhamen's tomb. These caskets are made of wood and bones.

Crole remarked, 'We should not forget that this is not an emperor's tomb. Nefrudet was a priest-cum-magician. One should be able to locate a lot of magic-related paraphernalia.'

My attention was now focused on a large box made of alabaster. Banister said, 'We'll open this box right now, but with real care and caution. As you can all see, there are hand-drawn pictures all around the box. The colours may come off if we rush.'

Bannister needs to be complimented for his patience. The more I see of this lad, the more I like him. After an effort of half an hour, not upsetting a single motif, he opened the lid. Focusing the torchlight on it one saw an assortment of jewellery, folded clothes and small statues in the box.

I peeked into the box. There was something shining inside. It wasn't gold. That this was a stone, of that there was no doubt. The stone was set in a shining metal. I asked Bannister, 'Can you figure out what that glittering item is?'

Bannister said, 'In ancient Egypt, the stones associated with gold jewellery were often semi-precious stones. That is, they were not very valuable. But semi-precious stones don't shine so much.'

'What would this suggest?'

'We need to be a bit more patient,' said Bannister. 'You might as well wait outside. I'll take out each item separately. And yes, no outsider should get any inkling about this stone. The reporters in particular.'

Crole and I came out. As this was lunchtime, we went looking for a bite. The reporters tried their best to extricate any information from us, but our lips were sealed. Till we get the green signal from Bannister we won't let out any information.

It will take a while for Bannister to bring out every single item from the box, and so nothing of great importance is likely to unfold. I couldn't have realized this sensitive exercise had I not seen this in person. Because it's a dry desert area things are still intact. Had it been elsewhere in the world, it would all have turned into dust as soon as it was exposed to the air.

An archaeologist from the Egyptian government, Dr Abdul Siddiqui, has started helping Bannister from today. Lord Cavendish is still in London; but he has stated that he will come over anytime, if necessary.

16 December

There can't be a more amazing discovery than this. The stone we saw glittering inside the casket turned out to be a diamond. Yes, a diamond, an item with which Egypt had no connection at all. Coming across a diamond in Egypt is as likely as a royal Bengal tiger in Africa! At the beginning of history, the diamond was exclusively an Indian asset. The presence of diamond mines in India goes back to antiquity. Whatever diamond has surfaced in the West has all come via India. After many centuries, in the eighteenth and nineteenth centuries diamonds were discovered in South America and South Africa. Even if the production of diamond has reduced in India now, the majority of ancient diamonds originate in India, starting from the Koh-i-Noor to other noted ones associated in its history.

But a diamond in Egypt! What startling news. The majority of the diamonds seen in jewellery here in Nefrudet's tomb are pea-sized, although some are a bit larger. All of these are set in gold. Laboratory testing has also revealed that these are all genuine. These can be compared with the world's best diamonds. In hardness and glow, these diamonds belong to the top category.

Needless to add, this news has spread like wildfire. This is a first in the history of Egypt's archaeological excavation. As of now everyone is clueless about how and where these diamonds came from. Trade with India is being mentioned as a possibility, but that India had gold 3500 years ago has not been established clearly in history so far.

Lord Cavendish arrived in Cairo soon after getting this news. Today we all met. A striking man of fifty, so full of life. To celebrate this extraordinary incident he threw a huge party in Karnak Hotel. As this happens to be a tourist season, there was no dearth of guests.

So far, seven diamond-studded necklaces and three pairs of earrings have been unearthed. I am sure many more are waiting to be discovered. The main chamber where Nefrudet's mummy is kept is yet to be opened. At the party, I spoke with Bannister about this incident. He looked baffled. A new chapter of history has opened up, something no one had ever associated with Egypt before. Still, the matter smacks of some mystery.

Bannister said, 'In the history of Egypt, one never found any connection with carbon. This country never ever had anything to do with coal. But the main constituent of diamond is carbon. There's no logic to this discovery as far as I can see.'

Tomorrow, another room will be examined. One hopes this will be the central room, where Nefrudet's coffin should be located. By now, the news of the diamond has appeared on the front pages of all newspapers across the world. The number of visitors at the dig's location is now out of control. After the diamond episode, the Egyptian government has also provided police protection at the site. Other than Lord Cavendish, his close associates and the two of us, no one is allowed to enter the tomb.

17 December

This morning I heard of an incident that may not bear any connection to the digging but is certainly related to diamonds. At present, all over the city, the topic under discussion is of course diamonds. One French resident of our hotel narrated this story to an avid audience.

About three months ago, Lord and Lady Ainsworth, a royal couple from England, had come and stayed at Karnak Hotel for a few days. Lady Ainsworth owned an immensely valuable diamond necklace in which the main diamond's size was that of a grape. This necklace had gone missing as had Lord Ainsworth's retainer, Francis.

The police think this could be the handiwork of the noted Greek diamond smuggler, Dimitrios Makropoulos.

He was spotted in Cairo three days before this incident. In the past, Makropoulos had gone behind bars twice. Clearly, this had not reformed him. The consensus was that he had acquired the necklace after bribing Francis. Hence, Francis too had to flee.

I thought to myself, thank God such robbers had spared Nefrudet's tomb. Otherwise, their loot would have been quite substantial.

At two o' clock in the afternoon, the seal of the third room was finally broken. Our predictions turned out right. This is the main chamber and herein lies Nefrudet's bier. His chamber turned out to be huge. It was filled with numerous small-sized wooden furniture. To start with, these were removed from the room. Nothing noteworthy was found.

It was decided that Nefrudet's own chest would be opened tomorrow morning. In general, these coffins have a covering of a wooden shell. Once these are removed, what emerges is an embellished covering of the mummy, the top of which shows the portrait of the departed person. Below this, one can see folded hands over the chest followed by the bottom part of the body and the legs. This entire figure is covered with artistic patterns and designs and the chances of coming across gold in the workmanship were high.

I am sure that by tomorrow afternoon Nefrudet's coffin will be exposed.

18 December

A bolt from the blue!

A necklace, holding an extraordinary sparkling diamond, was found on Nefrudet's portrait, covering the face. Bannister had entered the room a couple of hours before we did. When called upon by him, the first to go in were Lord Cavendish along with his two friends followed by Crole and myself. The comment Cavendish made after glancing at the necklace for a while wasn't a pleasant one. 'I must say, it looks exactly like Lady Ainsworth's diamond.'

There is of course a reason for this. The Egyptians had, even at that time, mastered the art of cutting diamond, something India never had a flair for. Hence, the look of this diamond was rather contemporary. Crole whispered into my ears, 'Magic, magic . . . this is nothing but magic.' I don't think there's anyone in Europe to match Crole when it comes to his faith in magic, mumbo-jumbo and so on. Crole has convinced himself that magic has a strong role to play in the way diamonds have manifested themselves in this ancient Egyptian tomb. He refuses to believe that a diamond can be made only through chemical reactions.

Whatever the case, the astonishment at seeing this 3500-year-old diamond will always remain unparalleled.

19 December

What a revelation! Didn't expect this to happen at all.

After examining the diamond in Nefrudet's necklace, the Cairo police have gone on record to say that it certainly belongs to Lady Ainsworth's necklace. A picture of the necklace was dispatched immediately to Lady Ainsworth, who recognized the diamond as her own. The theory of diamond production in Egypt 3500 years ago is now considered to be a complete hoax.

The Cairo police have also given an explanation of what might have transpired. Apparently, the day Lady Ainsworth lost her necklace, Makropoulos was not in Cairo at all. He was in Athens. He has a strong alibi. Hence, he has no role to play in this diamond robbery. As a result, the Cairo police have now arrived at a different theory. On the day of the robbery, they say, Bannister was in Cairo. He was staying at Karnak as well. It was he who bribed Ainsworth's retainer, stole the necklace and with his help produced a necklace with an Egyptian design and placed it inside Nefrudet's tomb. The entire point was to stir up curiosity. Howard Carter had earned a worldwide reputation after excavating Tutankhamen's mausoleum. Bannister wanted to outshine Carter in this regard.

Meanwhile, something else had happened. America's De Beers Company controls the entire world's diamond transactions. A representative of this company has come here to investigate the matter. If it were possible to create diamonds artificially, the diamond business would have gone to the dogs. Of course, when they heard that the diamond belonged to Lady Ainsworth, they felt relieved it had been found.

The police are questioning Bannister. Cairo Police is ruthless in such matters. Lord Cavendish has broken down completely. His mind is swinging between belief and disbelief. He told me that Bannister was fiercely ambitious, though one can't question his work. Both Crole and I are convinced that Bannister is innocent but how do we prove it? Even if he had indeed stolen Lady Ainsworth's necklace and created a fake copy of an Egyptian jewellery, he actually had the opportunity to put it inside the casket as he was always the first one to enter the chamber. We went only after him and that too a few minutes later! It's impossible to arrive at any decision on any precise plan of action right now.

In the meantime, the work of excavation has now been taken over by Dr Siddiqui. Lord Cavendish too has agreed to this arrangement. As we had become quite familiar with Siddiqui, the doors to the tomb remain open to us. Now, the question is: What happens if more diamonds are found? Will Bannister be declared a hardcore thief?

My inner self tells me no more diamonds will be found! And that's the problem. In the last few days, the amount of jewellery that's been dug out is huge. Yet, if no more diamond is found, it'll be very difficult to save Bannister.

Today I'm in no mood to even write my diary.

In the face of the police's brutal interrogation, Bannister has admitted to his crime. Now the law will decide on the sentence. I don't wish to stay here any longer. Crole too is in the same state of mind though today a fourth room, a small one, has been opened containing magic-related items. Crole said that after going through this just once he too would leave. I too have agreed to his decision.

22 December

That this episode will reach its end on this note was well beyond my imagination.

I have already mentioned that the majority of items in the fourth room were related to magic and chiefly comprised human skulls and animal bones. After sending these away, when the room became comparatively less cluttered, our focus fell on a medium-sized alabaster casket.

After opening the casket very carefully, Siddiqui said, 'I can see a papyrus scroll.'

After drying leaves from the papyrus plant, the ancient Egyptians used this as paper. The English word paper owes its origins to papyrus. The papyrus is processed and made into sheets which are then used as writing material.

One then wrote on these sheets with a pen and then rolled it up. This rolled-up sheet is called a scroll.

This present scroll was placed gently on a table, which was further covered by a sheet of glass, and then this papyrus roll was read. Needless to add, this was written in the old Egyptian hieroglyphics script. Siddiqui, Crole and I were all capable of reading this script.

It took three hours to spread this scroll evenly.

Then all three of us gradually read its content.

The excitement almost choked us. By the time we finished reading, beads of sweat had appeared on our faces and our pulse rates were soaring.

The name of Nefrudet was inscribed at the end of the scroll. Clearly, he himself is the author of this piece.

The text described the ways to produce diamonds.

It said that diamond production requires thirty-six different ingredients, all of which are freely available in modern Cairo.

The three of us looked at each other.

Siddiqui said, 'That means Bannister is innocent?'

I said, 'We still can't say that; this too can be a fake.'

'What then?'

'There's only one way out.'

'And what's that?'

'After organizing all the ingredients and following each and every instruction, you need to create diamonds in your own laboratory.'

'You're quite right.'

After working for nineteen long hours in the laboratory, the diamond we produced measured, even at its initial stage, equal to our Koh-i-noor. Though there was not enough time for cutting and polishing it, it came out in flying colours when examined for other regular tests. The police, Lord Cavendish and finally Bannister saw the diamond. When I saw him bursting into tears in joy, my eyes too swelled up with tears.

Bannister was released. The police once more began their search for Lord Ainsworth's retainer, Francis.

When all the hullabaloo was done with, in a formal ritual I took out Nefrudet's papyrus, shredded it into pieces and threw the pieces into the Nile.

No one will be able to use this formula, the knowledge of which is limited to only the three of us. We know too well that it's the scarcity of diamond that gives it value and appreciation. In some instances, there's a real need to protect the rarity of an object. And there's no doubt that the diamond is one such object.

4

Shonku and the Primordial Man

7 April

The newspapers have already reported on the amazing discovery of the anthropologist, Dr Klein. While travelling in South America's Amazon forests, he came across a tribe that still lives in the way humans did three million years ago. This is a crucial discovery. Not only that, just as an animal is captured for a zoo or a circus, Dr Klein too captured one such specimen in a cage from this clan and brought him home to Hamburg in Germany. I've seen an image of this person in the papers. It's quite difficult to make out any difference between him and an ape, although he walks on two feet. This prehistoric man lives inside a cage at Klein's residence. He consumes raw meat, cries out like an animal and doesn't use any language, and sleeps most of the time.

I had a great longing to meet this man in person; that this desire would get fulfilled is something I hadn't at all expected. Yet, this wish of mine will come true now. Yesterday, I received a letter from Klein. He writes:

Dear Professor Shonku,

As an inventor, you have an international reputation. All scientists across the world have deep respect for you. You must have read in the papers that I have with me a specimen of the ultimate prehistoric man, referred to as Homo afarensis. I'm keen that you come here once to meet this amazing man. I know that you travel to Europe at least once a year. Could you make a trip to Germany? If so, please let me know. Wherever you stay, I'm sending you a personal invitation to come over to Hamburg. All at my expense. I'd like to invite a few more scientists at that same time. Otherwise, none of you will get a chance to see such a primordial man in person. During my expedition I realized there were only twelve such men in existence. I don't think they will live for long. And the chance of others encountering them is also rather bleak as the way to those areas is very dangerous, full of ferocious animals. My young friend, the noted scientist Hermann Busch, fell off the boat into a river and turned into a crocodile's feast. It's a matter of great fortune that I have returned in one piece.

Whatever the case, please let me know about your decision soon.

Heinrich Klein

Here I must mention that I had met Klein's young colleague, Hermann Busch, five years ago in Bremen. He was an exceptionally gifted biologist. The tragic end to his life has haunted me since. I haven't had a chance to meet Klein yet. I've heard he is a fine gentleman. To his credit, he has produced numerous original works in anthropology.

I have received an invitation for a conference in Geneva this September. I was in two minds about going—not getting any younger, I can't suffer the stress of a flight any more—but I've decided to go to Geneva, all thanks to Klein's invitation. It's the opportunity of a lifetime. To be able to study a real living human instead of the fossils of human bones is a real stroke of immense good luck!

My problem is that if I leave in September, I may not be able to finish one task I've undertaken at present. I am conducting some experiments to prepare a drug, whose composition includes a compound called Alixirum. If this drug can be produced successfully, it will create a worldwide stir. According to my studies, this drug helps in speeding up evolutionary changes in a man by an incredible factor of a hundred thousand times. In other words, if a man is injected with this drug, within five minutes he will undergo an evolutionary change. Under normal circumstances, an evolutionary change takes place over a span of ten thousand years. I tested the drug on my retainer, Prahlad, which yielded no result. When I increased the dose of Alixirum and once again injected it into Prahlad, I witnessed him delivering a lecture on a subject of very complicated mathematics!

However, this state didn't last for long. Within ten minutes, he went to sleep. When he got up, Prahlad was back in his true form. He said, 'After you injected me, my head began to reel. I think I was talking gibberish. Isn't it?'

I don't think I can proceed any further for the lack of Alixirum. Last year I'd ordered a bottle of it from Japan. This drug too has been invented only in the last three years. It's a very potent drug, but expensive. The reaction I observed after injecting Prahlad with it has left me very satisfied and enthusiastic. There's no doubt that in the future the size of a human brain will increase manifold. In the next phase, due to constant dependence on machinery, the overall human body may become very frail but the presence of new drugs will induce the brain to increase in size. Of course, it will take a very long time to arrive at such a scenario. It could take 20,000 to 30,000 years. If I can successfully create my drug, there will be no need to predict the future; we will clearly see right before us how a human can transform.

I've replied to Klein's letter. I've also added that it would be a good idea if he could invite two of my friends, Crole and Saunders. They are both matchless in their respective fields. Crole is an anthropologist and Saunders is a biologist.

I'll be leaving by the second week of September. First to Geneva, then to Hamburg.

10 September

Today I'm leaving for Geneva. In the last few days, I have received letters from both Saunders and Crole. I'd informed Crole about my drug.

In his reply, he wrote:

Please bring along your drug in its current condition. Alixirum is available in many big cities of Europe. Klein himself may have it. It'll be quite thrilling to observe both the states of humans in the past as well as future all at the same time. I'm quite fond of that fellow Klein. I'm sure he'll allow you to use his laboratory.

I'm carrying a bottle of Evolutin to Hamburg. I would like to discuss this matter with Klein.

16 September, Hamburg

After finishing my work in Geneva, I've finally reached Hamburg. The other guests have also arrived. Apart from Crole and Saunders, there are the French geologist, Michel Ramon; the Italian physicist, Marco Bartelli; and the Russian neurologist, Dr Ilya Petrof.

I reached Klein's residence at night. After greeting me, he said, 'The humanoid sleeps early. I firmly believe that three million years ago the prehistoric men behaved exactly like this. Therefore, I'll take you all to meet him tomorrow morning.'

I didn't broach the topic of the laboratory and my experiments at all. I'll raise the subject after a few days here. But I didn't forget to offer my condolences regarding his colleague's untimely demise. That I knew him personally too is something I told him now.

There was no lack of hospitality during dinner time. Other than meeting my old friends, I enjoyed meeting three unknown scientists. Bartelli, Ramon and Petrof—all three are eagerly waiting to meet this prehistoric man. All of them agreed that this was an amazing discovery and that the Amazon is an incredible place.

Klein informed us that an eighteenth-century Spanish traveller mentioned this Brazilian clan in a rare travelogue. He observed that the breed fell between apes and Homo sapiens. This significant reference had particularly inspired Klein. His descriptions in the travelogue had enthused him to travel deep into the forests of Amazon. He had not at all envisaged that this journey will turn out to be such a success.

Petrof asked Klein, 'Have you made any attempt to civilize this man?'

Klein said, 'I don't think I can teach anything to a human who exists in exactly the same state as three million years ago. And the most amazing thing is that till now fossils of this kind of human were found only in South Africa yet I have located a real, living human in America.'

'How have you kept him?' asked Bartelli.

'Within my own compound I've created a space of 100 square yards enclosed by iron bars. He lives within that enclosure. I had no wish to keep him captured within a room or inside a cage. He seems quite happy to live in these natural surroundings. I'm yet to see any signs of him missing his brethren. I had to organize an armed guard for his security and protection. He hasn't shown any sign of aggression; but I know he possesses tremendous strength. He once snapped a thick branch of a tree with ease.'

'Have you noticed any emotional signs of grief or happiness in him?' I enquired.

'No,' said Klein. 'Occasionally he produces sounds similar to a gorilla's scream.'

'Does he walk on all fours at all?'

'No. There's no doubt that he is indeed a human. He always walks on his two feet. He eats fruits and vegetables; consumes meat too. But he eats raw meat, not cooked. He hasn't yet learnt the use of fire. Once, I lit a fire in front of him; he ran away, screaming.'

At 10.30 p.m., we returned to our rooms. One must admit our host is not lacking in generosity.

17 September, 11 p.m.

What a fantastic experience. We six scientists met a live *Homo afarensis* today. We would have taken him for an ape had he not walked upright on his two feet. His entire body was covered with thick brown hair. Klein has made him wear a pair of half pants, perhaps to bring in an element of civility and has provided him with a bearskin for the cold. So far, the human has felt no need for it. Klein has also kept water inside a hole on the cement floor. While we were there, the hominid drank water from it just like an animal. After noticing us staring at him, he hid himself behind a chestnut tree and moments later peered out with caution.

Klein has strewn the barred compound with pebbles of various shapes. The human took one in his hand and began to play with it.

Really, I had never imagined I would see such a scene even in my dreams. Petrof took some pictures with his camera. But the human never came closer than a distance of twenty yards.

In our presence, the armed guard brought raw beef in a plastic bucket and offered it to the human. While he ate, we all noticed the power of his jaws.

While having lunch Crole said something to Klein.

'I hope you've noticed that your human is left-handed.'

This is something I too had observed. He was picking up the stones with his left hand.

Klein said, 'Yes, I know. I noticed it on the very first day.'

Ramon said, 'This prehistoric man of yours sports an expression of intelligence—the way he looked in our direction . . .'

Klein shot back to say, 'Which means we cannot undermine the intelligence of *Homo afarensis*. He is certainly not a fool. When he started to use his two feet to walk, the size of his brain must have increased simultaneously.'

I put across my request to Klein to see his laboratory. He readily agreed. He said, 'Very well, we will visit it right after lunch.'

After lunch, Klein treated us to a very fine Brazilian coffee and then took us to his laboratory. It was teeming with a wide range of apparatus and medicines, suggesting that it could definitely carry out all kinds of experiments. What appealed to me the most were the three bottles of Alixirum placed together on a shelf on one side of the laboratory. Of course, I haven't told anything about my own drug to Klein yet.

After dinner, exchanging a few notes and finally bidding goodbye to each other, we returned to our respective rooms. Something was bothering me but I couldn't put my finger on it. Just then there was a knock at the door. I checked the time. It was 10.45 p.m. Who could it be?

When I opened the door, I saw Crole and Saunders. 'What is it?' I asked.

Crole said, 'The room in which I'm staying must have accommodated Hermann Busch once. Because I found his notebook in one of the drawers.'

'What's written in it?'

'What I read in it makes me very depressed. Even after traversing 350 miles through the jungles and the tributaries of the Amazon river, when Klein couldn't locate any prehistoric man he had almost given up. It was Busch himself who had encouraged him to go there. He had said that the description mentioned by that Spanish traveller could never go wrong. But—'

'But what?'

'There was some hesitation in Busch's mind. He could foresee that he wouldn't be able to see the end of this journey. He had often noticed that he possessed an uncanny power to predict the future. Klein had no such fear or hesitation; never ever feared for his own life. He was full of courage. Even while travelling on the ship he was continuing with his experiment.'

'What experiment?'

'That Busch doesn't disclose. I don't think Busch knew about this.'

'Poor Busch!'

As it is, Busch's death had upset me a lot and now this news added to that grief.

'Not just that,' said Crole. 'That Klein would become world famous after inventing something significant was what Busch could intuit. And that's precisely why Busch didn't want Klein to retreat.'

Saunders looked a bit preoccupied. I asked him what was bothering him.

He said, 'Nothing much. Just one doubt. I was under the impression that prehistoric men were small built but this one is almost 5 feet and 9 inches in height.'

I said, 'That's nothing to worry about. Even if he is prehistoric, he belongs to the twentieth century. It will be wrong to presume that all his signs will resemble that of a *Homo afarensis*.'

'That's true.'

It was getting late. Our discussion could not proceed further. Before leaving, Crole said, 'Now you must talk about your drug to Klein. You'll need his Alixirum. Hope he'll have no reservations about this.'

Tomorrow morning I will tell Klein about my drug.

18 September

This morning at the breakfast table, I told everyone about my drug, Evolutin. I also described the outcome of the experiment on Prahlad and finally I put forth my request to Klein. 'I think my experiment will achieve success if I get just one spoonful of your Alixirum. I'm ready to pay for it.'

I saw Klein look rather shaken with the news of my drug. He said, 'You speak about paying for a spoonful of Alixirum. What sort of a fellow are you? Forget about all that. Suppose you complete the work on your drug, on whom will you conduct your experiment? Who will be the subject? Where will you find him?'

I smiled and said, 'Why, there's always your *Homo afarensis*. If I experiment on him, he'll transform into a modern man, a Homo sapiens, within half an hour.'

I can't be too sure, but I thought I saw Klein's eyes gleam. He said, 'Have you also prepared its antidote to transform the man to his original state?'

Nodding my head I said, 'I've made arrangements for that too.'

'You're very thorough, I see,' said Klein. 'However, there's something I haven't spoken about. I believe in astrology. Today is not an auspicious day for such tests. I'll give you my Alixirum tomorrow morning.'

After breakfast, once again we went to see the prehistoric man. Today he seemed a lot less inhibited. He came within a range of a few feet and looked at us. He looked closely at me for almost two minutes. Then he made a rough sound though that didn't carry any sign of anger.

I still can't shake the doubt off my mind. Every time I encounter this special example of *Homo afarensis*, something starts bothering me. Yet, I can't explain in words exactly what it is and why. It could be that with age my thinking capacity has reduced.

18 September, 10 p.m.

Ever since dinner, I've been feeling queasy; perhaps saying just queasy will be wrong. My head is spinning and I can hardly think straight. I'm carrying with me my own invented medicine, Miracurall. After taking a dose of it, I returned to my normal self.

Suddenly, there was a knock at the door. It was Saunders and Crole again. Something was amiss. Crole said, 'During dinner something must have been mixed in our drinks. My head is reeling and my thoughts have all gone awry.'

Saunders said, 'I too am in a very similar state.'

I gave each of them a dose of Miracurall and soon they were back to their normal selves.

But what may have happened to the other three?

We ran to their rooms with the medicine. After forcing their doors open, we gave my medicine to each of them. Each one was in a similar state. Petrof knows English quite well, speaks with us strictly in English yet he was speaking in no language other than Russian, that too with grammatical errors. Bartelli was also incoherent and constantly repeating the words, 'mamma mia . . . mamma mia', while our French friend was silent, staring in front of him with a glazed expression. However, thanks to my medicine, in no time each one returned to their normal state.

The question is: What does one do now? Is Klein after us for some reason? But why? Did he want to disrupt my work in his lab? But why attack everyone else in that case?

There was no point in pondering over it right now. We returned to our rooms.

Almost immediately, I realized that I ought to create my drug Evolutin as soon as possible.

But with the current equation with Klein, will he offer any help at all?

This is something we won't get to know before tomorrow morning.

19 September

This morning when we went down for breakfast, Klein spoke first. 'Were you all all right last night? I was severely indisposed. I feel there was something wrong with the food.'

Of course, we admitted that we too were unwell but felt better after taking the medicine.

'Which medicine did you take?' enquired Klein.

'A medicine made by Professor Shonku,' said Saunders.

'Oh, I see! Had I known, I too would have taken it,' said Klein. 'How I suffered the whole night. Only after six in the morning did I feel the worst was over.'

'That reminds me, if I can get Alixirum today I'll put it to use in my work,' I said.

'Very well, I'll give it to you right after breakfast.'

After breakfast, Crole, Saunders and Petrof went out for a stroll. Bartelli and Ramon said they would like to click a few photographs of the prehistoric man. As he had shed his fear and comes close to us, good images were possible. I stayed there for a while, watching him play with the pebbles with his left hand. I could not explain why it bothered me.

I went to the laboratory along with Klein. The moment Klein lifted the Alixirum from the shelf I realized the bottle had been tampered with. The look and the smell was not that of Alixirum. Alixirum gives a hint of light blue but this one was as clear as water. It had obviously been diluted. I have worked extensively with the solution, and it's not that easy to fool me.

I didn't let on that I had made out the tampering. I quietly took out a spoon of the liquid and put the lid back on the container.

I felt dejected and returned to my room. The possibility of my experiment succeeding had been snatched from me at the last moment. What more regret can there be? I could look for it at any pharmacy in town, but what's the guarantee that Klein won't jeopardize my plans?

At 10.30 there was knock on the door. I found Saunders and Crole in front of the door.

'Have you got the drug?' asked Saunders.

I replied, 'Yes, I have but it's not the real thing. It's spurious.'

'I thought as much. Here's your Alixirum.'

Crole took out a bottle from his pocket and gave it to me.

What a relief that was! Instantly I mixed a spoon of Alixirum to my own medicine.

'But on whom would you like to try this out?' asked Saunders.

On someone who might help unravel a huge mystery, I said. But not right now. Later tonight.

Despite Saunders and Crole's pleadings, I didn't disclose my plans.

During lunch, Klein sent a word to say he was feeling unwell and that we should pardon him and have lunch without him.

In the evening, we went out to see the Hamburg city. When we returned at 7 p.m., we were told that Klein had recovered, had gone out but would be back by dinner.

I couldn't fathom why, but a shiver ran down my spine. Klein had gone out! Alone or with someone?

Looking at the others I said, 'I fear a disaster. We must check if the prehistoric man is still inside the enclosure. Just wait for a minute while I bring along my own weapon because you never know what catastrophe is about to strike us.'

I don't always carry my Annihilin pistol with me when travelling but this time I had, for some inexplicable reason. After taking it out from a box, we all ran towards the enclosure housing the cage.

One has to open an iron gate to enter the enclosed area. Just in front of the gate stands an armed guard, Klein's confidante Rudolph. He took out his revolver the moment he saw us. Left with no choice, with the help of my Annihilin I had to eliminate him along with his weapon.

Now we had a clear road ahead. Six of us entered the cage. Checking out the area for a couple of minutes we realized the prehistoric man wasn't there. In other words, Klein had left, taking the hominid with him.

Crole displayed his presence of mind. He went straight into the house and called up the police. I remembered the number of Klein's Daimler car. Crole gave that number to the police and asked them to apprehend the car right away.

It took twenty minutes for the police to get back. The car had been flagged down between the Königstruss and Grünberg crossing. Klein had killed a policeman with his revolver while resisting arrest. The police also said that Klein was accompanied by a wild man. The two had been taken to the police station. We were to report there at once.

After booking two taxis over the phone, we reached the police station after a short drive. Klein was being interrogated. We wanted to meet the wild man. A constable took us to a room inside. The only furniture there was a chair and a table. The *Homo afarensis* was in one corner of the room, all curled up on the floor, sleeping.

Taking out a packet from my pocket, I proceeded towards the sleeping figure. The packet contained all the items required for an injection along with my own drug, Evolutin. I put the drug into the syringe and injected it into one of the arms of the sleeping man.

We waited for a reaction.

Within five minutes, we began to see the various stages of transformation. The hair on the body began to disappear; the temple widened; the jaw shrank; the eyes came forward in the socket; the muscle index of the body reduced.

Within fifteen minutes we realized that the person we were looking at right now didn't belong to any Brazilian clan; he was of European origin; the colour of his skin was like all my European friends. His hair was blonde, his age couldn't be beyond thirty, and judging by his profile and eyes he looked very handsome.

'Mein Gott!' cried out Crole. 'This is Hermann Busch!'

I gave him another injection to arrest the metamorphosis back to the *Homo afarensis*. When I nudged him, Busch jumped up, rubbed his eyes and asked us in German, 'Who are you? Where am I?'

I said, 'We're your friends. Your enemy is now under judicial custody. Why don't you tell us exactly what experiment was Klein conducting on you?'

'Oh!' Busch struck his head. 'He was preparing the drug of Satan.' On its application, the person would have moved backwards in evolutionary terms. 'On the basis of a complete lie, Klein took me to Brazil. At an opportune moment, while we were on the boat on the Amazon, he gave me that injection at gunpoint. I've no further recollection of what happened to me. But you . . . I recognize some of you. You're Professor Shonku, right?'

'That's right. Now I want to ask you a question.'

'What is it?'

'You're left-handed, aren't you? You had written down your name and address in my diary once. I remember that.'

'Yes, I'm left-handed.'

It was this that had haunted me and made me restless since the first day I had seen the wild man.

*

It's so amazing, both Klein and I were scientists involved in the same area of experiments, although he was moving backwards and I forward. There's no escape for Klein. He is condemned to a long term in jail for the death of the policeman.

As for me, with the wisdom of hindsight I feel it's best not to tamper too much with evolution. Let nature take its own course. The bottle of Evolutin may as well showcase its presence only on a shelf in my Giridih house. There's no question of me using it ever again. Yet, one must admit that it produced such amazing results when put to use.

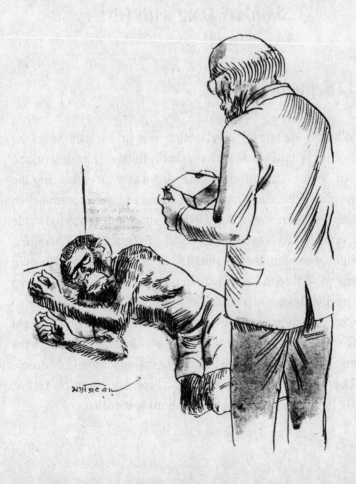

5

Shonku's Date with History

12 September

What a delightful day! After one-and-a-half years of relentless hard work, we have finally finished all our work on our device. Though the entire idea was mine, I'm using the word 'we' because by no means could I have accomplished this task on my own. My Giridih laboratory cannot provide the necessary material to build this machine. Therefore, right at the initial stage, I had written a letter to my German friend, Wilhelm Crole, who in turn wrote to the well-known Psychic Research Institute in Munich, Germany. Thanks to Crole's recommendation, we received a grant in financial aid from the institute and it became possible for two Germans and one Indian scientist to create this machine in Munich. The second German is a young fellow, one Rudolph Heine. He has an insatiable curiosity about spiritualism.

Now, let me say a few words about the machine we invented. We have called it Compudium. That is, computerized medium. Those who connect with departed souls in a séance often take the help of a medium, an individual through whom the spirit communicates with this world with ease. Spiritual mediums possess a special quality. I have come in contact with many mediums in my country and have studied them carefully. There is something special about them. They are sensitive, sharp, emotional and always preoccupied or absorbed. They often suffer from indispositions and many die young. Before we completed this machine, both Crole in Europe and I in India studied the characteristics and behaviour of at least 350 mediums in detail. Our sole mission was to set up a mechanical and artificial medium to establish contact with the spirit world in place of a real live medium. Thanks to the generous endowment from the Psychic Research Institute, there was no stopping us in our quest. The results our Compudium has yielded so far confirms that our joint effort is nothing but a grand success.

The machine need not have resembled a human but we decided to give it the shape of a body and add a head to it;we have also added a pair of legs to make it stand. The equipment is a metre in height. We have created a slit on top of the head to insert the name and details about the spirit one is going to call upon. This equipment will be placed on one side of the room and the people taking part in the séance will be seated about two metres away facing the machine. After inserting the card in the machine, the lights are switched off. In this pitch-dark, a red light fixed in the machine's chest will gradually come on, indicating that the spirit has arrived. Now we start asking questions and the answers begin to emerge from the mouth of the machine. When the spirit begins to feel tired, the red light will gradually fade out and the séance session will come to an end.

The three of us have tried out our tests on this machine. Adolf Hitler's spirit was called. Within a minute of inserting information about him, the red light glowed.

I asked him in German, 'Are you Adolf Hitler?'

The reply was 'Ja', which means yes in German.

Crole asked a second question: 'Don't you have any regret or remorse for torturing and killing the Jews so ruthlessly during your lifetime?'

Immediately, a shrill voice came out in the form of a reply from the machine, 'Nein, nein, nein,' that is: 'No, No, No'. This encounter went on for about five minutes.

This experiment proved two things: One, that it worked! And two, that it was clear that Hitler's opinion of himself had not changed even in death.

We will take a break for two days and then resume our work on the machine. Heine's aspirations are very high. He thinks if we can further fine-tune the machine we can even see the image of the spirit. In other words, the spirits will appear before us in person.

That would be very useful, an added bonus; my latest invention has already reached a state which is definitely quite unprecedented in the history of science.

Now we need to select a few scientists and invite them over for a demonstration of this machine. So far, the news of the invention is yet to reach the public.

At Crole's request, I'll stay back in Munich for another month.

15 September

With the help of this machine, we were able to connect to two more spirits of well-known personalities. One is an Indian, Nawab Siraj ud-Daulah. This was chiefly to satisfy my own curiosity. I checked with Siraj about the Andhakup murder (Black Hole of Calcutta, 1756). With a lilt in his voice, Siraj said he knew nothing about this and that the British had spearheaded this horrible campaign only to malign him! Spirits do not lie. Hence, in my mind at least, his honour was restored with ease.

The second spirit was that of Shakespeare. My question to him was: 'There are some who are of the opinion that judging by the standard of your education and your modest family background, it doesn't seem plausible that you penned these plays and poems. Many people are of the view that the real writer is Francis Bacon. What's your opinion on this?'

To start with, the spirit of Shakespeare, after hearing my question, let out a hearty laugh. He then recited a charming four-line poem on people's lack of faith and respect and asked me, 'Do you know what the name Bacon means in my language?'

I said, 'What?'

'Bacon means country bumpkin. Go and check any dictionary. You will find the meaning. And this country bumpkin is supposed to have created my plays? Have people lost their minds?'

During these last two sessions, only three of us were present. Last evening, we invited eleven scientists. We gave them a demonstration of the machine. Crole had forewarned me about the presence of a few scientists who don't believe in a spirit world. He mentioned Professor Schultz in particular. Even as a person, Schulz doesn't have much of a reputation though he is heading a physics-based organization. When its former director Professor Hubermann suddenly died three years ago, Schultz was offered this position.

I said, 'A few sceptics who will be difficult to convince doesn't bother me. We'll carry on with our demonstration irrespective of Schultz.'

Heine said, 'The best way to convince them would be to call upon Hubermann's spirit. All present are familiar with his style of speaking. If our machine adopts that similar style, it will be easy to convince them.'

We agreed to his suggestion.

Everything was arranged in a hall of the Psychic Research Institute. The séance was fixed for 7 p.m. Everyone arrived on time.

Before settling down in a chair in the front row, Shultz said, 'I'd like to see the machine first.'

Crole said, 'Gladly.'

Shultz scrutinized the machine in great detail for five minutes. He then returned to his own chair and quipped, 'It's fine. The farce can now begin.'

Crole announced that to begin with we would try to establish contact with Professor Hubermann. I had assumed Schultz would raise some objection to this, but he remained quiet. The others present agreed to the suggestion.

After putting the required information into the machine through the slit in the head, Crole switched off the light and occupied his seat next to me.

Each one in the room was watchful and quiet. Even the sound of the fourteen scientists breathing could not be heard.

After two minutes, the light started shining. In the radiance of the light partially reflected on the people, all of us could be easily identified. But the area behind the machine was completely dark.

'Are you Professor Hubermann?' enquired Crole.

A voice responded, 'Yes, but why have I been called? This fake world holds no value for me.'

'Why do you say so?'

The answer was, 'What's the point of a world where even the most brutal murderer gets away from the law?'

I noticed the guest scientists stirring with excitement. Schultz roared, 'What's all this rubbish? Crole, I'm convinced that you're speaking on behalf of Hubermann. You're adept at ventriloquism!'

That Crole knows ventriloquism is something I too was aware of. But there was no doubt that this voice was indeed emerging from the machine. Crole's mouth was shut. It's simply not possible to voice words without opening one's mouth.

Meanwhile, words once more started coming out of the machine.

'I was the director of a physics-based organization. To grab my position, Johann Schultz mixed potassium cyanide in my coffee. For the sheer lack of evidence, he went scot-free. What can be worse than this? I . . .'

Suddenly, there came the sound of smashing glass and the light went off. My eyes were on Professor Schultz. I had seen him take out a pipe from his pocket and hit the light of the machine with it to smash the bulb.

With the fading of the light, the words from the spirit died out too.

Crole got up and switched on the lights.

All our eyes were on Schultz. It was obvious that he had nerves of steel. He pointed to Crole and said coldly, 'On the basis of today's incident, I can call for a defamation case against you. Projecting the machine as an excuse to prove I'm the assassin? What audacity!'

He strode out of the room, leaving behind his pipe.

Out of those who remained, only one, a physicist, Professor Erlickh, commented in an intense voice: 'Today, Hubermann's spirit has confirmed most of our reservations. This machine is incomparable.'

18 September

The reputation of our Compudium has reached far and wide. We need to organize one more demonstration. In the meantime, we have fixed another bulb. Our young friend, Heine, is spending a lot of his time on the machine so that some more qualities can be assigned to it. On next Saturday, 22 September, fifty cognoscenti have been invited to witness a demonstration. It will take place inside the institute. The invitees comprise noted scientists, writers, doctors, musicians, artists, businessmen, journalists—people from all walks of life. Let's see how this works out.

23 September

What a ruckus! Don't know how to deal with these journalists. Despite a legitimate demonstration and hard-core proof, the journalists claim it is a fraud. According to them, we get into action in the dark and insist it's the machine's work. 'Three scientists' tricky device', 'Disgrace to science' were some of the headlines which appeared in the newspapers.

Heine insists, 'Unless you provide the spirit in person in front of them they won't be convinced.'

We have given him one month's time to work on this aspect. If he meets with success, nothing like it.

Now let me recount what had happened at the gathering on 22 September.

But before this let me tell you one more thing.

I was toying with the idea that in the recent past we have related to the spirits of the civilized world; how about moving further back in history? It struck me after I came across an article recently published in a journal. A historian by the name of Baumgarten, while commenting on the Stone Age, stated that whatever colourful images one has seen of animals in the caves of Spain and France are impossible to conjure even by contemporary artists. And that these can in no way be accomplished even by artists of the Stone Age. While reading this article I remembered that when these caves were discovered, people had claimed that these pictures, said to be 20,000 years old, were in fact drawn by modern-day artists!

I decided that this time, with the help of Compudium, I would call upon the spirit of a Stone Age person. Of course, there's no question of speaking with this person as at that time language was yet to evolve. However, to see how this spirit behaved, if he produced any sound from his mouth—that in itself would be a learning experience for us. He might start speaking in an unknown language. That of course would be a valuable discovery for us.

Crole agreed to my proposal and added, 'In that case, we must also invite the article's writer, Baumgarten . . . let him be present.'

I agreed and said, 'An excellent plan.'

After getting in touch with Baumgarten, I realized that he not only dismisses the Stone Age cave paintings, but that he is also a staunch sceptic about séances. Only after much persuasion and cajoling did he finally concede to our request.

On the 22nd at 7 p.m., everyone gathered at the institute's medium-sized hall. The machine was placed against the windowless large wall. All of us, including the invitees, sat around it in a semicircular position, maintaining a distance of about two metres from the machine. Before the session began, I stood up and announced that this evening we were going to invite a spirit from the Stone Age. In case this produces no response, we would call upon a spirit belonging to the prehistoric age.

I now inserted the relevant information inside the machine. Needless to add, the machine works on electricity. The room was plunged into darkness. We continued to sit in anticipation. It was now well beyond three minutes, and no lights were showing. Did that mean . . . No . . . we could finally spot a flicker of light.

Eventually, the voltage of the red light increased, before stabilizing.

No sound. I could, however, smell something wild. This must be Heine's work of art. Hitherto, there had never been any smell.

After waiting for a couple of minutes I asked in Spanish, 'Has any spirit arrived in this room?'

Instead of a reply in any spoken language, we heard a rattling wild sound. This was followed by some more similar sounds that we couldn't decode.

We realized it was pointless communicating with this spirit.

What does one do now? The red light indicated the presence of the spirit.

The light glowed for the next ten minutes before fading out.

When the lights were turned on, everyone present in the room exclaimed in different capacities at the amazing scene we witnessed.

The white wall behind the machine showed a colourful image of a charging bison with a horn covering the entire wall. Picasso would have been proud of himself if he had drawn this picture.

The unknown 20,000-year-old spirit from the Stone Age had left behind this work of art.

28 September

After that extraordinary episode, one of our viewers, the archaeologist Professor Weigel, gave an interview in the papers praising our machine to the skies. At the same time, Baumgarten labelled us as bogus in some other paper. Apparently, one of us—Crole, Heine and I—is an artist and taking advantage of the darkness had drawn that figure in that wall. This has resulted in endless raging debates in various papers.

The majority of the tabloids are against us. Disgusted with this breed of journalists, I have been contemplating returning home. However, Heine appeared suddenly this morning and declared jubilantly that he had succeeded in his mission at last—the spirit had started appearing in person next to the machine. This left me speechless. When Crole was informed, he said, 'We need to check on this right away. What have you tested?'

'How could I make this up?' jibed Heine. 'I've just now spoken to my namesake, the eighteenth-century poet, Heinrich Heine. I can even describe in detail the dress he wore.'

We instantly sat down to study the machine. Within ten minutes, we saw the world-famous German composer, Beethoven, clad in a black suit pacing up and down right in front of us. Before we could shoot a question at him,

Beethoven lamented, 'Oh God—my deafness will be the end of me! How could you destroy my hearing ability?'

I remember Beethoven had turned deaf since his middle age.

We were of course thrilled with Heine's achievement. My inner self tells me perhaps one can now alter the rigid mindset of the journalists and prove the uniqueness of this machine. We decided that taking the institute's help we would call for another meeting inviting all journalists, particularly the ones who had criticized our efforts. This time we would use the bigger lecture hall of the institute and place the machine right in the middle of the platform.

With this in mind, we sent out all our invitations. We also invited Schultz. He phoned me after receiving the card. He said: 'So what new charade have you planned this time?'

I remarked, 'Why don't you witness everything with your own eyes? All I can say is that this time it will be not just an aural experience but a visual one too.'

Shultz laughed and retorted, 'But then who doesn't enjoy watching such magic? And if one can divulge your tricks publicly what can be nicer?'

I calmly said, 'Even if this be your ultimate aim, do come, please.'

'Let's see,' said Schultz.

I have a feeling that Schultz can't help but come.

In all we invited 700 people. The hall can accommodate 800.

The meeting is scheduled for 3 October.

4 October, 12.30 a.m.

It makes me shudder again and again every time I think of the last evening's affair. There's no doubt that we were victorious all the way. After the meeting, despite the climax, no one could refrain from clapping. The Compudium did full justice to our efforts.

All the invitees had come. Who wants to let go of an opportunity of watching a spectacle free of cost! Before the meeting, Crole gave an introductory speech to explain our mission. Judging by history, no one had easily accepted any of the revolutionary scientific discoveries. Starting with telegraph, telephone, television to nuclear explosion, men landing on moon, sending satellite into space—people have nursed their reservations about every innovation. We too would face a similar reaction and what was about to be demonstrated would now perhaps instil faith in people's mind concerning our machine. That is what we hoped for.

It was decided that Heine himself would insert the information inside the slit of the machine and would not disclose the identity of the spirit to anyone. Not even to the two of us. It would be a complete surprise. Crole and I agreed to this scheme. Though he is young, Heine is a very promising scientist; and he has the ability to think on his feet, an ability which is always valuable especially during this kind of experiment. After Crole finished his speech and sat down, Heine stood up and welcomed everyone present in the audience. He said, 'We have informed you all that we will call upon a spirit with the help of our Compudium. All I want to say is that I'll not reveal beforehand whose spirit will appear now. When the spirit arrives you can see it with your own eyes.'

Heine took out a card from his pocket and inserted it inside the head of the machine. He then indicated to one of his workers to put out the lights.

I don't normally get nervous or restless, but for some reason I felt as if my heart was skipping a beat or two. Whose spirit would appear at Heine's call?

Nothing for five minutes. Pitch-dark room. All the windows were draped in black curtains. Someone controlled his cough. Silence once more. I could feel everyone waiting with bated breath.

My attention was fixed towards the middle of the platform.

Hey ho . . . I thought I could perhaps spot a red dot.

Yes, no mistake. A red light glowed from the machine's heart. Does that mean . . .

I suddenly heard a sound in the silent hall.

The sound of a storm.

No, not a storm. A flying pair of wings of a bird.

There's the bird. Is it a bird? The one flying across the entire hall. What is it?

I finally comprehended we could see the bird because of the shining phosphorous on its body. A cross between a bat and a reptile, this being emerged from the middle of the room and was circling across the hall, while producing a cry through his mouth wide open, baring his pair of fangs.

Pterodactyl!

This fanged and ferocious creature had existed on this earth fifteen million years ago. Heine had put in this description in the card. This creature's eyes were sparkling green, the very symbol of aggression. On top of this, the light emanating from the body added an even more dangerous edge to the vision.

There was much chaos in the hall. Sheer terror.

Drowning all noise, Heine shouted into the mike, 'Are you convinced now?'

The response echoed in unison across the hall, 'Oh yes! Please remove this being. Right away.'

Heine must have switched off the machine's light. The other lights came on in the hall.

Amongst the present audience, seven had fainted in fright. A black-suited man in the front row had even fallen down from his chair.

When I went close to the figure I realized it was Professor Schultz.

Holding his wrist and checking on his pulse, Crole blurted out abruptly, 'He is no more.'

Against this backdrop of death was an incessant clapping.

'Hail, Compudium! Hail, Science!'

6

Shonku and Frankenstein

7 May

Yesterday, I received a letter from Germany written by my English friend, Jeremy Saunders. It bears an amazing piece of information. I reproduce the letter here.

Dear Shonku,

I'm in Augsburg, Germany, holidaying with our mutual friend Crole. After my arrival here, I received a remarkable piece of news. I'm sure you have heard of the renowned scientist of the eighteenth century, Baron Victor Frankenstein. When Mary Shelley wrote her novel entitled Frankenstein, *people were of the opinion that Frankenstein was a fictional character. But it has recently come to light that there was indeed a real scientist by the name of Frankenstein who, like Mary Shelley's*

Frankenstein, had invented ways to revive a dead body. I'm sure you also know that the story shows how just one small mistake led to Frankenstein creating a monster instead of a human. Well, one of this Baron Victor Frankenstein's descendants actually lives close by—in the city of Ingolstadt. We're thinking of meeting him one day. If he has retained some of his forefather Baron Victor Frankenstein's papers that would be incredible. We both would like you to join us. Augsburg is going to organize a science conference and we can make sure that you get an invitation from them. They will bear the travel expense. Please let us know of your decision soon. Hope you're keeping well.

With best wishes,
Jeremy Saunders

I did not waste any time in replying with my consent. I visit Europe at least once a year. So far, I hadn't made any plans to go there, so this is as good an excuse as any to travel. That apart, who doesn't know about Victor Frankenstein's incredible discovery as well as its dismal consequence. He definitely succeeded in giving life to a dead person but as he had, apparently mistakenly, inserted a murderer's brain into the dead person's head, the resurrected human took the shape of a violent and virulent demon. Ultimately, a fire consumed the demon.

One could hardly find any presence of a scientist who could match up to Frankenstein's talents in the eighteenth century. It'll be a great achievement indeed if we can find his papers. But do these papers still exist? I have my doubts.

21 May

The invitation from Augsburg has arrived. I'll leave this Saturday, 25 May. I have no idea of what the future holds for us. Even if one doesn't get to locate Frankenstein's papers, I feel very happy at the prospect of meeting two of my dearest friends, Crole and Saunders.

27 May

I reached Augsburg yesterday. Both my friends are indeed very happy to have me over. The science conference continues for three days. Then on the 31st we'll go to Ingolstadt. In the meantime, we have found out the address of Baron Julius Frankenstein. Schloss Frankenstein, i.e., Frankenstein Castle, is the name of his house. The Baron is apparently an art connoisseur who boasts an enviable collection. My desire to meet him has increased manifold.

2 June

Yesterday we arrived in Ingolstadt. We left after breakfast in Augsburg and travelled by road, arriving at our destination well before lunchtime. Ingolstadt is an old city and strikingly beautiful, like a picture postcard. It's located along the banks of the Danube. Quite a few old castles dot the cityscape. There's also a university.

We booked three single rooms in a small hotel. After having lunch, we scanned the telephone directory and located Frankenstein's number. Crole called him right away. Fortunately, we got him on the phone. He too had just finished his lunch. After introducing himself, Crole said, 'I along with my two friends would like to meet you in person. Is that possible?'

Frankenstein readily agreed. He invited us to his house for tea at 4.30 p.m.

We took a taxi and arrived at the castle gates on time. The words Schloss Frankenstein were inscribed in German in marble on the large gate. We drove down a long cobbled driveway for a while till we arrived at the main door of the castle. An elderly uniformed retainer opened the door and welcomed us into the house. We walked into a large hall. A spiralled wooden staircase went up to the first floor on one side of the hall. The moment we sat down on a velvet, upholstered sofa, a handsome, middle-aged man climbed down the staircase and greeted us, saying he was Julius Frankenstein. We introduced ourselves. When he realized I was Indian, his face glowed. He said, 'I have many books on Indian art and many collections of Indian art. Hopefully there'll be an occasion to show them to you.'

After this, the gentleman took us to the drawing room, more a resting room. The walls were adorned with paintings by famous European artists and portraits of various personages, perhaps Frankenstein's ancestors.

We sat down and within minutes another retainer arrived, rolling in a trolley on which were arranged tea and pastries.

We realized Frankenstein knew English rather well and therefore chose English as our medium of communication. Crole initiated the conversation. 'We are all scientists. I'm a geologist, Saunders an archaeologist and Shonku is an inventor. Each one of us knows about your ancestor, Baron Victor Frankenstein. We have read about him and are aware of his research and its results. My question is: Is anything left of his papers, documents, notes, formulae?'

After keeping silent for a brief spell, Julius Frankenstein smiled and said, 'Victor Frankenstein was my great-grandfather. Both my grandfather and father were scientists; only I never went in that direction. But I haven't allowed a single paper to be destroyed. Not just that—even his laboratory remains as it was in his day. His own leather-bound diary has been preserved with great care. But you understand . . . it's now over 150 years. One needs to go through the diary with great care; the pages tend to tear easily.'

Saunders asked, 'Can we see the diary?'

'First finish your tea,' said Julius Frankenstein, 'then I'll show you the diary.'

My heart trembled at these words.

We spoke of many other things while sipping tea. One topic left me very disturbed. Julius Frankenstein said, 'It's a matter of deep regret that a past event of Germany has once more raised its head in Ingolstadt. Have you heard of Hans Rudel?'

Crole said, 'Yes, I've heard of him but does he live here?'

'Yes, he lives here,' said Julius Frankenstein.

'I believe he is a Hitler supporter. He is trying to spread Hitler's line of thoughts among the public. He has also established a group.'

'All this is true,' confirmed Julius. 'And the most appalling thing is he is once more trying to rouse anti-Jewish sentiments.'

Due to Hitler and other leaders, millions of Jews were shipped to concentration camps in the 1930s and '40s. The Second World War ended with Hitler's fall and with that the persecution of Jews.

'Aren't you Jewish?' asked Saunders.

That any name ending in 'stein' denotes a Jewish name is something I was aware of.

'Yes, indeed,' said Julius Frankenstein. 'The members of Rudel's group come home and threaten me at gunpoint to extract money at regular intervals. But I'm not the only one. A lot of wealthy Jews in Ingolstadt are being targeted. No one can match up to Rudel's despicable nature. He alone leads this group. The other members of this group are hooligans by nature but Rudel is educated as well as intelligent. An anti-Semitic stance runs deep in his veins.'

This news distressed me no end. The very thought of Germany once more facing harsh times saddens me immensely.

We finished our tea. Julius Frankenstein said, 'Now let me show you the diary.'

He led us to the library, a room lined with book-filled cupboards and shelves with large books on art.

Julius Frankenstein took out a key from a drawer and opened a chest. With great care, he took out a packet wrapped in silk cloth. He peeled the cloth away to reveal a leather-bound book with gold inlay work on the cover. By book I mean the diary.

'These are my great-grandfather's notes. Mentioned here is the procedure he followed in reviving a dead body as well as his first experiment and its tragic consequence.'

The paper looked fragile and the ink was faded, but the beautifully handwritten notes in black ink could still be read clearly.

'Was this formula used again by your father or grandfather?' I asked.

'No,' said Julius Frankenstein, 'after that unfortunate incident no one ever touched this book.'

'Marvellous!' All three of us were completely taken in by this astonishing experience. It was all so overwhelming. So many years ago, one scientist could actually accomplish such a task. How remarkable.

'How many people are aware of this notebook?' I asked.

'No one else,' said Julius. 'But the knowledge about my great-grandfather's invention and its results are universally known.'

We had to accomplish one more task. Study Victor Frankenstein's laboratory.

Our host took us down a long, twisting passageway and opened a door to let us into a room.

How incredible! This huge laboratory, the equipment, still intact even after 150 years! What a range of machinery Victor Frankenstein had produced in that age.

We spent a few minutes looking around and then took our leave. How much I desire to read that diary, but that was not to be. We thanked Julius profusely and returned to our hotel.

12 June, Giridih

Yesterday, I returned home from Augsburg. The sight of Frankenstein's diary now seems like a dream. The one thing I can't stop thinking of, unfortunately, is not a dream; it's a harsh reality. The Hitler-centric Hans Rudel's dreadful deeds. Hopefully, he will be tackled soon. Otherwise, doomsday is here. In Germany as well as the rest of the civilized world.

17 June

I received another letter from Saunders today. With very crucial news.

Dear Shonku,
You must have heard of Dr Thomas Gillette. There was no one to match this cancer specialist in the entire world. I'm saying 'was' because this morning at 7.30, Dr Gillette died following a heart attack. He was on the verge of inventing a sure cure for cancer. He had told me last month, 'Just another month, then there will remain no fear of cancer.' But before he could invent this cure he has left us. Nothing can be more unfortunate. I've written to Crole too. My wish: to go to Ingolstadt and ask Julius

Frankenstein to let us use his great-grandfather's diary to revive Gillette. Please let me know your views on this as soon as possible. I've asked the body of Gillette to be preserved in a cold storage. I've also shared my plan with the medical fraternity. They all agree with my plans.

With best wishes,
Jeremy Saunders

I've informed Saunders that I'll be leaving for Ingolstadt day after tomorrow. This time I'll bear my own expense. If this mission is accomplished, the matter of expenses is a small one.

20 June, Ingolstadt

We managed to convince Julius Frankenstein. In fact, he seems happy that his great-grandfather's notes will finally come to good use after such a long time. I said, 'But first I'd like to read the journal thoroughly. I need to understand the procedure well.'

Handing over the diary to me, Julius Frankenstein said, 'I've full faith in you. I know you'll return the book without any damage.'

At present, I'm alone in Ingolstadt. Today I will call Crole and Saunders. They will arrive tomorrow morning.

Saunders is responsible for transporting Dr Gillette's body to the Frankenstein mansion.

One thought is bothering me. As per Victor Frankenstein's formula, one needed to insert someone else's brain inside the dead body's head. This is a bit confusing. If someone else's brain is put inside Gillette's head, he will no longer remain Gillette. He will begin to function according to the rejuvenated brain. That's why Victor Frankenstein's human became a brutal murderer. I feel one needs to alter the formula. The plausibility of this will be confirmed only after I have read the whole diary.

21 June

I finished reading the entire diary last night. Not just that—I stayed awake the whole night and worked on all the changes required in the formula. If Gillette comes back to life, he can now continue with his work as he will now be using his own brain. I've introduced a slight change in the formula. Victor Frankenstein's formula was dependent on natural electricity. We don't have the luxury of waiting for a stormy day with lightning. I have thus invented a strain of high-voltage electricity that can be transmitted into the dead body. Let's hope the revised formula works. If successful, the formula need not be confined to Frankenstein's name alone; it can be redefined as the Frankenstein–Shonku formula.

23 June

Saunders, along with four other persons, arrived from London last night with Dr Gillette's body. Crole arrived this morning. The work begins today. In the meantime, Julius Frankenstein and his retainers have made the laboratory spotlessly clean for our use. All the apparatus looks almost new.

Ever since my return, I have found Julius Frankenstein very preoccupied. When asked about his anxiety, he said that the Hans Rudel group had killed one of his dear friends, Boris Aaronson, also a Jew. Aaronson was a professor of philosophy and apparently a real gentleman. Rudel used to harass Aaronson in many ways. Not being able to take this any more, Aaronson wrote an article severely criticizing the activities of Rudel and had it published in a newspaper. Rudel had him killed in revenge. He had organized it with such ingenuity that the police were unable to intervene in this matter. 'Killed by an unknown assailant' is how it was reported in the papers. Yet Julius and the rest of the Ingolstadt Jewish community knew too well who was responsible for this dastardly deed.

Notwithstanding this unfortunate incident, the Baron continues to help us. He knows the procedure on Gillette's dead body will begin this evening. Procuring the chemicals is not a problem as none of the necessary items is difficult to find. The uniqueness of Victor Frankenstein's formula was its simplicity. Saunders and Crole will, of course, help me. Apart from this, we have also engaged two local assistants—with great difficulty, I must admit. After ten individuals refused to work with us, we finally found two who agreed to work on the experiment. Everyone knows of the demon created by Baron Frankenstein; the locals all think we too are on our way to creating another one.

24 June

Experiment successful!

After tiring and exhausting work for seven-and-a-half long hours yesterday, we observed the first sign of life in Gillette's body this morning—a slight tremor in his right arm, on his lips and his eyelids. We were all breathless with tension by then. After half an hour, Gillette opened his eyes. He moved his eyes restlessly in all directions. The first words he uttered were: 'Where am I?'

I removed the strap from Gillette's hands. Gillette slowly sat up. Then he asked, 'For how long have I been sleeping?'

Saunders said, 'Seven days, Thomas.'

Gillette spoke as if he hadn't died at all. He said, 'Amazing. And here I've left my work incomplete. If I get two more days, I can finish my work on the medicine.'

'You can start your work from tomorrow,' said Saunders. 'At present you're in Germany. We have woken you up in a laboratory in Ingolstadt.'

I said, 'Please rest in bed for a while. We will bring some food for you.'

I can't tell you how content I felt. Julius Frankenstein was standing right next to me, shaking my right hand with both his hands. I said, 'Today I can see, as a scientist, how far-sighted your great-grandfather was.'

26 June

What a horrifying experience.

We sent Dr Gillette back to London in a completely normal state. Along with him, the other four men who had accompanied Saunders also returned. Julius Frankenstein requested all three of us to stay for few more days. 'I haven't yet shown you my art collection,' he said. 'Please shift to my house. There's no dearth of rooms in the castle.'

That's exactly what we did. Yesterday, Julius Frankenstein showed us his Indian art and sculpture collection. What an amazing array of Mughal and Rajput paintings Julius has collected. He said he'd been collecting these over the last twenty-two years.

Julius is an impeccable host. We were revelling in all sorts of comfort; eating good food, strolling around the gardens surrounding the three sides of the castle.

The incident took place at 10.30 in the morning. The four of us were sitting and chatting together in Julius Frankenstein's drawing room. Suddenly Julius's retainer, Fritz, rushed into the room, his face pale and his hands high in the air. He was followed by four hooligans, each one brandishing lethal weapons.

'Raise your hands!' The leader of the gang roared. Left with no choice, we complied.

The leader of the group now faced us. 'We have heard that a doctor from London has been gifted with a fresh lease of life. We are aware of Baron Frankenstein's exploits but we didn't know his equipment is still fit to be used to revive a dead person. We hear it has been done recently. That is why we are here. Our leader Hans Rudel died at 5.30 this morning. Thrombosis. We want him revived. In fact, we order you to revive him. If you do not concede to this, none of you'll be allowed to live. Even Baron Frankenstein's equipment will not be able to revive you, as we will attach stones to each of your necks when you die and drown you in the Danube. Now let me have your views.'

Julius Frankenstein was livid with anger. 'Remember, if you harm us in any way you will not escape the police.'

Hissing like a snake, the rogue in the front said, 'If you utter one more word, we'll shoot you. Now tell me, when can we bring Hans Rudel's dead body here? Remember, if you don't honour our request, none of you'll be able to return to your own countries and Baron Frankenstein too will not get any protection.'

What does one do! Our hands are tied. I said, 'Please bring Rudel's body to the castle this evening. We need to prepare ourselves before that. But he won't be resurrected before the day after tomorrow as the arrangements are a little more complicated.'

Once more, the group of hoodlums threatened us and then left. Julius Frankenstein said, 'What a grave mistake it was to report Gillette's news to the media. If it hadn't been publicized, they wouldn't have got wind of it. With Rudel's death, the pro-Hitler followers would have dispersed. Ingolstadt would have seen the end of anti-Jew uprisings.'

26 June, 12 a.m.

I can't sleep a wink. The mere thought of conceding defeat to such a vicious gang is poisoning my mind. Do we have a choice? I have a plan, though its result cannot be predicted beforehand. Yet we are left with no other option. For this, we need the active help of Julius Frankenstein. If this works out, it will benefit one and all and I'll come out as a champion! In the past, I have managed to cross many unthinkable hurdles, but this will be my real acid test.

28 June

First, let me recount in detail the story of Rudel's resurrection.

Following our instructions, Rudel's men brought his body to the Frankenstein Schloss the day before yesterday. Going by his looks, one couldn't guess his violent and ruthless nature. He was average to look at, not more than forty years of age. I asked the men to place Rudel's body on the steel table in the laboratory. I then said, 'You all now return the day after tomorrow, early in the morning. I've full faith that Rudel will have come back to life by then. But if you surround us with guns every minute, there's no way we can function properly. You have to trust us. If, when you return the day after tomorrow morning, you still find Rudel lifeless, you can take any action you deem fit. Since one dead body has come back to life I see no reason why it won't work this time.'

Fortunately, Rudel's followers believed us and left.

Here I must mention that I regret I'm not carrying my lethal weapon Annihilin with me as I had no idea that I'd be facing such danger. With Annihilin, it would have been so easy to wipe out the entire gang in an instant.

After Rudel's men left, I turned to Julius Frankenstein. 'Do you have any surgeon here who can operate on the brain? He should be very competent.'

Julius Frankenstein said, 'Yes, indeed. Heinrich Kümmel is Germany's most noted neurosurgeon. I know him quite well.'

I then revealed why I posed this question.

'I want to revive Rudel adopting the same method as used by Victor Frankenstein to reincarnate dead bodies. Therefore, in this case I require a brain to be inserted in place of Rudel's brain. I need to discuss a few things with you but strictly in confidence.'

I didn't want to disclose this to Crole and Saunders right then and hence I took Julius Frankenstein to the next room to discuss my plans. Julius promised all his help. I have to depend on Julius Frankenstein as we are strangers in this town. Also, as an inheritor of a great heritage, he can exercise his influence.

We had to give our dinner a miss tonight. Both Saunders and Crole are as excited as little boys. They said, 'Why aren't you revealing your scheme to us?'

I responded, 'I myself don't know what result my tests will reveal. To an extent, it's a shot in the dark. But both of you will bear witness to whatever happens the day after tomorrow.'

The next day Dr Kümmel arrived along with his colleagues, carrying a glass case with a brain immersed in spirit. By 11.30 in the morning Rudel's brain was taken out and replaced with this brain. I've rarely seen such a neat as well as quick surgery in my life. Kümmel said he would waive any fees in exchange for the chance to see the whole experiment through till the end. We, of course, agreed to this instantly.

Sharp at noon our experiment began at the Victor Frankenstein laboratory. Deep inside I began to pray. What if a human is replaced by a demon! I've no idea what will happen.

After working all through the night, at seven in the morning, we could see signs of life in Rudel's body. And the first question Rudel asked in German was the same as Gillette's: 'Where am I?'

I leaned forward and told him in German, 'You were asleep for the last four days. Today you've woken up. At present you're in Baron Julius Frankenstein's laboratory.'

'Julius Frankenstein?'

'Yes.'

I hadn't noticed till now but suddenly I observed many people in the room. Right behind us were standing two of Rudel's men, carrying revolvers. Seeing Rudel alive, their eyes opened wide!

At this point, Rudel's attention focused on these men. He said, 'What's going on? What are they doing here?'

This response was peculiar. One of the hooligans foolishly said, 'I'm Emile, Herr Rudel, a member of your group!'

The other fellow too followed him and said, 'I'm Peter, Herr Rudel, your follower!'

The resurrected Rudel growled, 'Get out of my sight. You all are part of a notorious group. Because of you, Germany is once more going down the drain. Just get out of my sight. Right now.'

The rogues Emile and Peter left the room looking thoroughly baffled.

Now both Crole and Saunders confronted me. 'What's going on? Tell us all.'

I said, 'First let me make sure Rudel gets a proper rest.'

I fed orange juice to Rudel and put him to bed. Then I turned to Crole and Saunders and said, 'Without Julius Frankenstein's help this experiment wouldn't have been possible.'

'But whose brain was put in Rudel's head?' asked Crole.

I said, 'Boris Aaronson, who was killed by the Rudel group. Julius Frankenstein obtained permission from Aaronson's son and the police to exhume the body from the grave. Dr Kümmel then extracted his brain and transplanted it into Rudel's skull. He has transformed into a new person. He is no longer his former self. Perhaps this pro-Hitler group will now vanish into oblivion.'

Julius Frankenstein was so moved that he had tears in his eyes. Once more, he took my hands in his and said, 'Germany will forever remain grateful to you.'

I said, 'The entire thing was executed by your forefathers. If anyone deserves any thanks, it should be Baron Victor Frankenstein.'

13 July

After returning home, I received a letter from Julius Frankenstein. He informed me that nowadays Rudel introduces himself as a Jew. His group has fallen apart; the people of Ingolstadt are once more living a secure life devoid of any fear.

7

Dr Danielli's Discovery

15 April, Rome

What a remarkable incident. I'm here to attend a science conference. Yesterday we had a lecture by the local biochemist, Dr Danielli. He dazzled everyone. Maybe I'm not as impressed as the others; but I will elaborate on this further.

Before I comment on Danielli's work, I need to mention one thing. Many of us know of the novel *Dr Jekyll and Mr Hyde*, written by the famous English writer, Robert Louis Stevenson. For those who are not familiar with it, let me explain the premise of the story. Dr Jekyll was of the opinion that each person has two sides to him—a wise one and a wicked one. A person tries to conceal his vices because in order to exist in a society one has to observe a set of rules. But Dr Jekyll had claimed he could invent a drug that, if consumed, would bring that individual's vile qualities to the fore and turn him into a violent creature. According to the story, when no one took Dr Jekyll seriously, he invented the drug in his own laboratory and tried it on himself, transforming himself into the violent Mr Hyde. Mr Hyde went on to commit a murder as well, although Dr Jekyll was otherwise a real gentleman.

The novel by Stevenson created a great impact, but no one has been able to produce such a drug. Danielli declared he was about to do so, but I must mention that before Danielli I had already created a similar drug in my laboratory in Giridih. I haven't consumed it myself but I have tried it on my pet cat, Newton. I gave the cat a drop of it and within three minutes he attacked me fiercely and scratched my right hand. I've called my drug 'X'. At the same time, I've also invented its antidote, 'Anti-X', which after consuming this, the affected subject can return to his former self. Even after I gave Newton the antidote, it took me some time to calm him down.

During Danielli's lecture, his own persona had almost turned into Mr Hyde. I'd met Danielli soon after arriving here and found him very sober and courteous in nature. But I guess he had been provoked; at least three scientists—England's Dr Stebbing, Germany's Professor Kruger and Spain's Dr Gomez—strongly opposed his views. This resulted in chaos at the meeting.

It became very difficult for Dr Danielli to retain his composure. After a long time have I witnessed such a commotion in a science gathering. Danielli said his medicine would be ready in a couple of days' time. And he also announced he intends to test it on himself, just as Dr Jekyll in Stevenson's novel had done. This doesn't appeal to me because if this experiment is indeed a success, we really can't predict how much Danielli will change after consuming the drug. After having witnessed first-hand what happened to my cat Newton, I've developed a deep fear of such an experiment. Of course, I haven't disclosed the invention of my own drug to Danielli or anyone else for that matter.

The delegates' lunch will be served in half-an-hour. We have all been put up at Hotel Suparba, which is also the venue of the conference. The lunch will be provided in the dining room on its first floor. The seminar continues for another two days. I'll stay on in Rome for two more days before returning to my own country.

17 April

I met Danielli after the summit. I said I firmly believed in what he had said in his lecture. I also added that I too hold the same view. This gave him tremendous joy and encouragement. I said, 'I hope you're also inventing a drug to cure the ill effects of the drug you're preparing.'

'Yes, of course,' said Danielli. 'In this connection I'm deeply influenced by Stevenson's novel. I've no idea why no one else ever thought of producing such a drug.'

I said, 'The reason behind this can be found in Stevenson's novel. If such a drug creates an individual like Dr Jekyll, one can easily infer the danger of using such a drug.'

'But that doesn't mean science should come to a halt,' quipped Dr Danielli. 'We ought to continue with our experiments. If I am indeed successful in my experiments, notwithstanding its outcome, one has to admit that it'll be a landmark in the world of science.'

'But if you turn into Mr Hyde, I won't approve of it personally.'

'Let's see what transpires.'

'May I please know what exactly has gone into producing this drug?'

The response I received left me very excited.

I too have created this medicine using these exact components.

I, of course, didn't reveal this information to Danielli and he too didn't disclose the exact measurements of the ingredients.

18 April

Dreadful news in today's newspaper.

Dr Stebbing is missing.

Our hotel is situated on the River Tiber. Apparently, Stebbing went on a walk along the river each night before dinner. Today too he had gone for his walk but he did not return. The police fear that he may have been accosted by a gangster who killed him and threw his body into the Tiber.

I have a different conjecture, however. Stebbing had taken a very strong stand against Danielli's lecture and addressed Danielli as unscientific. Danielli had clearly mentioned that within two days his medicine would be ready.

After consulting the telephone directory, I located Dr Danielli's address as 27 Via Sacramento. Without further delay, I called for a cab and headed towards his home.

It was no problem to locate his house but I was told he wasn't in. Danielli's retainer opened the door for me. He asked me, 'Would you like to speak with Signore Alberti?'

'Who's he?'

'He is Professor Danielli's colleague.'

I said, 'Very well, call him then.'

The retainer seated me in the drawing room and left. Within a couple of minutes, a thirty-year-old young man appeared in the drawing room. Black hair, black eyes, intelligent looks.

'Are you Danielli's colleague?'

More than colleague, I think it would be correct to call him his assistant; he was so young. 'I've been with Dr Danielli for the last three years. Are you the Indian scientist, Prof. Shonku?'

I said, 'Yes.'

The lad's eyes sparkled. He said, 'I've heard a lot about you. I've read about all your inventions. I feel so proud to meet you.'

I said, 'I'm happy to hear that. But I'm here to meet Dr Danielli. When will he be back?'

'Any moment,' said Alberti. He has gone to the market to buy a few things. Why don't you sit for a while?'

I decided to wait. To while away time I asked Alberti, 'Has the professor finished his work on the drug?'

'Yes, he did so the day before yesterday,' said Alberti. 'Ever since, the professor has started looking very preoccupied. I've noticed a subtle change in him. But I won't be able to explain further what exactly this change is.'

'Has he consumed this medicine?'

'I cannot tell. He alone has created this medicine. I wasn't involved in the process at all. I have no knowledge of the formula either. He did inform me that the medicine was ready.

But this is something I would have gathered anyway, because all of last month he would lock himself up in the laboratory. It's just in the last two days that he hasn't done any work.'

The doorbell rang. Soon, Danielli entered the room, carrying a packet with him.

'Good morning, Prof. Shonku. This is a very pleasant surprise!'

I wished him good morning. 'I hope you don't mind my arriving unannounced.'

'Oh, no, not at all. You're most welcome. Now tell me . . . what news of you?'

'It's you who should have the news of your medicine. Is it ready now?'

'Yes, indeed. In fact, only the day before yesterday.'

'Have you tested it?'

'I had one teaspoonful of it.'

'And?'

'I've no recollection.'

'What does that mean?'

'My head reeled and I fell down unconscious. When I woke up in the morning, I found myself on my bed. There was no strain in my body. I've no knowledge of what transpired last night.'

'Have you read about Stebbing's demise in today's paper?'

'Yes, indeed. I was very sad to see the news. Though he had disagreed with my theories, he was a scientist of a high calibre.'

'Have you arrived at any decision about Stebbing's death?'

'It's clear local miscreants are responsible. I believe after killing him they dumped the body in the Tiber. I guess it will surface in a few days.'

I didn't waste any more of Danielli's time. After thanking him, I returned to my hotel in a taxi. I'm still immersed in the thoughts of Danielli taking his own medicine. It's so strange that he could remember nothing. Will my own medicine also produce such a reaction? Newton had fiercely attacked me; did he do so unknowingly?

19 April

Yesterday around 11.30 p.m., Professor Kruger and Dr Gomez were found murdered in their rooms. At the same time, the body of Stebbing surfaced in the Tiber River. The throat of his body bears deep marks of fingerprints. In other words, he was throttled to death.

I have no doubt that all three murders were committed by none other than Danielli. The police of course are now investigating the case. Both Kruger and Gomez haven't lost any money. Therefore, it's not a matter of any robbery.

After questioning the receptionist of our hotel, the police have learned that at 11 p.m., a disgusting-looking man arrived at the hotel asking for the room numbers of Kruger and Gomez. And then called both of them up.

'Did you hear what he said?' the police asked.

'No, sir, I didn't hear anything else.'

Like Stebbing, both Kruger and Gomez have been strangled to death. There's no doubt left that the assassin is very strong and powerful. Yet when you see Danielli, you notice nothing strong about his physical appearance. And he is no less than sixty years old.

I called up Danielli at his residence. He himself picked up the phone. His voice was calm. There was no sign of any nervous tension or excitement. He greeted me most amicably when he heard my voice. I said, 'I need to meet you.'

'Come over right away,' said Danielli. 'I'm home the entire morning.'

Within ten minutes, I arrived at his house. He shook my hand with great affection and asked me to sit down. 'So how're things?'

I sat down and asked him, 'Did you consume you medicine last night also?'

'Yes,' he said, 'and experienced the same reaction. I've no recollection of what I did after taking the medicine, where I was, when I returned . . . I remember nothing.'

'You took a spoonful of this?'

'Yes.'

'You know that both Kruger and Gomez were murdered last night and also that Stebbing's body has been found?'

'I do.'

'All three of them had vehemently disagreed with you at your lecture.'

'I know this too.'

'Will you listen to me now?'

'What is it?'

'Don't take this medicine any more. Since you don't feel anything after taking the medicine, why have it? From the scientific point of view, you're not gaining any further knowledge. In fact you get to comprehend nothing.'

'That's true. But there's no doubt that something is happening.'

I took a deep breath. 'Don't mind my saying this,' I said, 'but I feel you are responsible for all three murders. That is, your medicine is responsible.'

He stared at me, shocked. 'Nonsense!'

'No, it's not nonsense. I'll tell you how I know. I invented this very same medicine in my own country, in my own lab. I tested it on my pet cat. I put a drop of it in his mouth with a dropper. Within three minutes, he attacked me and injured me. But I managed to give him the antidote, which too I had invented, and within half an hour he was back to his normal self.'

Danielli remained quiet for a few seconds. He began to breathe heavily. Then in a controlled voice he said, 'You invented this medicine before me?'

'Yes.'

'I don't believe you.'

For the first time I noticed a trace of bitterness in his voice. He once again said, 'I don't believe this.'

I said, 'You may not believe me but the fact remains it's true. You have mentioned the contents of this medicine but never revealed its quantities. I too have created this medicine using the same formula and I clearly remember its exact quantities. I'll repeat them to you now. Just check if this matches with your formula.'

I narrated the formula to Danielli. His eyes opened wide. Then in a measured tone, he whispered again, 'I don't believe this. The amount we've used is exactly the same.'

'So now you know.'

'You've never consumed your own medicine?'

'No, and will never do so.'

'But I need to take it. Till I come to know exactly what it's doing to me, what I'm up to, I am compelled to take this medicine. If necessary I may increase the dose.'

I looked at him. 'You really can't comprehend what you do after you take this medicine?'

He was getting agitated with tension. 'The first day I couldn't follow a thing. I've a vague recollection about yesterday. I know I left home and had got into my own car.'

'Do you have a driver?'

'No. I drive myself.'

'You can't remember what happens thereafter?'

'No. But in due course, I'm sure I'll get to follow what I'm doing, what changes I'm going through.'

'The outcome of this will not be a very pleasant one, Danielli.'

'Even so, for the sake of science I need to go through this. You and I are not the same individuals. My level of curiosity is much higher than yours.'

I realized my request to Danielli had fallen on deaf ears. Danielli would not listen; he was possessed by some devil.

I wished him a good day and returned to my hotel.

In the present scenario, I must make a decision quickly. In the last two days, three men who antagonized Danielli have been murdered. God alone knows how many more enemies he has? If I am right, how many more will die?

20 April

The report of the fourth murder has appeared in today's paper. Someone has strangled Rome's renowned physicist, Dr Bernini, while asleep at his own house. The police have some fingerprints and are investigating the murder.

I was completely baffled. Another murder! And why?

After waiting till 10 a.m., I called up Danielli's residence and asked to speak with his assistant, Alberti. When Alberti came on the line, I said, 'Can you please come over to my hotel? I'm in room 713. I have to speak with you on a topic of great urgency.'

Within fifteen minutes, Alberti was at my hotel.

I got down to my concerns straightaway. 'I've got this horrible suspicion that Danielli is behind this present set of murders. That he is committing these crimes after taking his medicine. What do you think?'

Looking grim, Alberti said, 'I too have formed this view since last night as those who have been killed have all at some point rebuked Danielli, didn't believe in his words or otherwise had protested against his views.'

'But the gentleman who got murdered last night . . . who is this Bernini fellow?'

'He is a noted physicist. He had once objected strongly to one of Danielli's articles and had written an article rebutting Danielli's thesis some three years ago. This had appeared in a journal.'

'So Danielli hadn't given up on his pent-up anger.'

'That's what I feel too. Rome has many such scientists who at some point of time have attacked Danielli in various capacities. Professor Tucchi, Dr Amati, Dr Mazzini . . . how many more names do I need to mention? I'm of the view that Danielli has nursed his grudge against each of them for years. He hasn't done anything till now because he is basically a very decent and gentle man. But this medicine is turning out to be his nemesis.'

He thought a bit and then asked me, 'I think you have produced this same medicine before the professor, haven't you?'

'How do you know?'

'Yesterday, I was having lunch with the professor. He himself said so and from his clipped manner of speaking, I don't think he is terribly happy with you.'

'Is that so?'

'Yes . . . and I suggest you look after yourself. Please don't let anyone enter your room at night.'

I shook my head.

'Meanwhile, these crimes will continue to occur. And with little pretext Danielli could now even start killing innocent people.'

'What's to be done?'

After some thought, I felt I had worked out a strategy. I asked him, 'Do you go to the professor's laboratory?'

'Yes, I do. Why not? I go during the daytime.'

'Is the medicine within your reach?'

'No. He keeps the drug locked inside his cupboard. The key is with him at all times.'

I pondered over it for some more time. Then I added, 'Do you live in the same house?'

'No. I arrive by ten in the morning and leave at six for my own house.'

'Do you have the keys to the laboratory?'

'Yes, I do.'

'Then at night we both need to enter his laboratory. We need to make sure that he no longer consumes that medicine.'

'Tomorrow I'm leaving for Milan. I'll come to you in the evening day after tomorrow.'

'Fine. We'll stick to this plan.'

Alberti left. We should have addressed this today, but it's not to be. I definitely require Alberti.

21 April

Today's papers have reported two more murders. Alberti had named one of them yesterday. The other one is Professor Bellini, a well-known biologist. Both had been strangled to death last night. The fingerprints found at the crime scenes match those found at the earlier murders. The police have finally realized that all these murders are being committed by the same person. Bellini's retainer has told the police that he heard the doorbell ring at 11 p.m. and when he opened the door he found a hideous man standing there. When asked, he gave his name as Arturo Croce. Croce asked to meet Bellini. Bellini still hadn't retired for the night, so he agreed to meet the visitor. Croce left after fifteen minutes; Bellini's retainer brought him his coat and hat and saw him off. When he noticed that his master had still not gone to bed, he peeped into his room and found him lying on the floor—dead. He immediately informed the police. The police found the assassin's fingerprints on Bellini's throat but are yet to locate the killer.

23 April

I don't have it in me to describe last night's horrible incident, yet I will do my best to write this down now, while the event is still fresh in my mind.

Yesterday, I'd gone out with a group of tourists. I returned at 4.30 in the afternoon. Then after having coffee, I walked on the banks of the Tiber for half an hour.

At 8.30 p.m., Alberti came to my hotel. We had dinner together. We decided to go to Danielli's house at 10.30 p.m. We were going to observe the house from outside. Since one can see the laboratory from the road, we would know when Danielli entered the laboratory. Accordingly, we would enter his house.

Danielli's neighbourhood is rather quiet, and more so at night. There's a park right in front of the house. We stood next to the railing of the park and decided to wait. The laboratory was dark; yet the other rooms of the house were all lit.

There's a church within 200 yards of this house. After five minutes of the bell chiming at 10.30, the lights of the laboratory were turned on.

Alberti and I now approached the main door and pressed the doorbell. The servant opened the door. The moment he saw us, he said, 'You can't meet Signore Danielli right now. He has left instructions.'

He had just about completed his sentence when Alberti punched him in the face and rendered him unconscious. We stepped over the body and entered the house. Alberti said, 'Follow me.'

The room next to the staircase leads to a long dark passage that eventually reaches the laboratory. The door was slightly ajar with lights from inside the laboratory spilling over into the passage.

I whispered to Alberti, 'I'm going inside. You remain outside the door; if need be I'll call for you.'

I entered the laboratory. Danielli had his back to me but I could see him measuring out some liquid from a bottle into a spoon.

'Danielli!' I shouted.

Hearing my voice, he instantly turned around, raised his eyes and said, 'Hey ho! You have come here? I was anyway heading towards your hotel.'

He lifted the spoon and swallowed what was in it. The transformation was instantaneous.

Gone was that gentle-looking scientist. In his place was a being—half human, half animal, a fierce look on its face.

Without any warning, he lunged at me. I moved at the speed of lightning and was able to avoid him and reach his table. In that split second, an idea struck me. As Danielli raised his hands to leap at me, I took the bottle from the shelf and consumed its content at one gulp.

All I can recollect now is pouncing on Danielli with a new and awesome might. We landed on the floor, wrestling like mad dogs. I do remember another thing. The medicine gave me the energy of a demon. I remember nothing else.

When I regained my senses, I found myself lying on my hotel bed. My whole body was aching with a pain I feel will never end. Right then Alberti entered my room.

'As you won't be able to leave the bed to open the door, I took the key from the room boy to open this room . . . hope you won't mind.'

'Good morning,' I said, moaning.

'How do you feel?'

'There's no injury on my body; but the pain is unbearable.'

'I've informed a doctor. He will examine you.'

'But what happened last night?'

'I saw two vile demons fighting to death. I don't know what would have happened if I hadn't come to take your side. At one time, I was into boxing. I knocked Danielli out with an upper cut. You had meanwhile managed to get a grip on him rather well. After he lost his senses I brought you to your hotel. When I put you to bed, you still hadn't regained your normal self. I stayed with you till I could spot my familiar Prof. Shonku. Then I returned home. It was 12.30 a.m.'

'And Danielli?'

At that very moment, a doctor arrived. After examining me, he asked me, 'Did you fight with anyone last night?'

I said, 'Yes, this young fellow knows the house . . . 27 Via Sacramento. Dr Enrico Danielli. He has rendered me in this state thanks to his drug. If you match the fingerprints found on the bodies of the scientists who have been murdered in the last four or five days with that of Danielli's fingerprints, you'll see they are the same.'

'Then it becomes a police case?'

'Certainly.'

'I'm reporting to the police right away.'

The doctor left soon after prescribing medicines for me.

Alberti now took out a bottle from his pocket. 'This is what remains of Dr Danielli's drug. Please keep this. Please place it next to the one you have invented.' He placed it on the table and smiled at me. 'I do hope you get well soon.'

I tried smiling back but it still hurt. 'I'm now under medication. So not to worry. I feel I can return to my own country by the day after tomorrow. Many thanks for all your help. I'll never ever forget you!'

8

Prophecies by Don Christobaldi

6 September

I just received an amazing letter from my English friend, Jeremy Saunders. I reproduce it here:

> *Dear Shonku,*
>
> *I have a piece of remarkable news which will be the highlight of this letter. The news has appeared in all the newspapers of our country but I don't know whether it's been carried in the papers in yours. It's like this.*
>
> *A very old manuscript was discovered in a library in Madrid about three months ago. It took all this time for Spain's noted linguist, Professor Alphonso Beretta, to decipher the manuscript. After which he announced his find at a press conference. The author of the manuscript is Don Christobaldi and the writing spans*

the years 1483–90. That is, 500 years ago. According to Beretta, Christobaldi has talked about numerous predictions, the majority of which have proven accurate. You must have heard of the Frenchman Nostradamus's prophecies. Nostradamus was born in AD 1503 and he too had predicted many events, many of which have come true: London's plague and fire; the predicament of emperor Louis XVI during the French Revolution; the rise and fall of Napoleon; groundbreaking invention by Louis Pasteur; the nuclear bombing over Hiroshima and Nagasaki during our lifetime; the abdication of Edward VIII from the British throne; the emergence of Hitler and many other things . . . Nostradamus had predicted these with great precision. But Nostradamus's predictions pale in comparison to this Spanish document. Not a single world-famous historical event in the last five hundred years has escaped Christobaldi's scrutiny. I'm convinced that he has even mentioned you: 'There'll be an emergence of an extraordinarily talented scientist in the twentieth century whose name starts with 'S'—who else can this be but you?

I went to Madrid recently and met Beretta and thoroughly discussed the manuscript with him. The moot point of writing this letter is to indicate a particular prediction by Christobaldi. He has written in one place: 'In the middle of the seventeenth century, an animal will appear in an island in the Pacific Ocean, which will be far *ahead of the progress that man has achieved in the field of science in the last 300 years. Humans will encounter this being in the second half of the twentieth century and it'll be humans who will make sure that this breed doesn't go extinct.'*

Now the question remains: Is there really such a being? Furthermore, if this is true, where did they come from and if its habitat is only an island, how could it make such a marked progress in the domain of science in such a short span of time?

During the seventeenth and eighteenth centuries, many well-known globetrotters travelled around the Pacific Ocean and discovered many things. I spent the whole of last month in the British Museum and read up interesting travelogues by these travellers. But one came to my particular notice. At the end of the eighteenth century, the French globetrotter Jean François de La Pérouse took a voyage to the Pacific Ocean. And he has left the description of a very interesting episode during this voyage. Apparently, La Pérouse's ship faced a violent storm and deviated from its normal course and reached an unknown island. It was dusk. At this very moment, La Pérouse witnessed a strange scenario. From one part of the island, a light beam rose and reached an unknown destination long away. La Pérouse never found out the reason behind this and when the storm subsided they returned to sea.

This description of what seems to be a lighthouse clearly reminded me of LASER (light amplification by stimulated emission of radiation). No other form of lightcanbe focused in thismanner. Imagine, this scene was witnessed a hundred years ago and the laser beam is a very recent discovery by humans!

Now, I'm very keen to go to this island and investigate further. I also strongly feel that Christobaldi's prediction of this creature is accurate. Remember the boat we used for our Munroe Island expedition? Our Japanese friend, Hidechi Suma, had created the jet-powered Sumacraft. We can use the same vehicle this time too. I don't think Suma will refuse us. And Crole is forever eager for an adventure; one is now left with only your consent. After all, I have known you for the last seventeen years and I'm convinced that you'll agree to this and join us in this new adventure.

Let me know of your decision soon as we need to work on various logistics.

With best wishes,

Yours,
Jeremy

Saunders is quite right about my enthusiasm. Could it really be true that superior beings who are not humans exist on this earth? Will Don Christobaldi's prediction be proven true? By us?

Of course, I'm all ready to participate in this expedition and I'll let Saunders know this today.

13 September

I've completed all my arrangements for the voyage. Suma enthusiastically agreed to lend us a craft. But we'll be using an advanced version this time—the Sumacraft-II.

Apart from the four of us—Saunders, Suma, Crole and myself—another person will form part of this expedition. He is Barcelona's renowned archaeologist, Professor Salvador Sabatini. I'd met him once during a science conference held in Brussels. He is not more than sixty; there's no doubt about his scholarship, though he can be a bit conceited and stubborn. He has read Christobaldi's manuscript and what amused me was that he is of the opinion that the noted scientist 'S' whom Christobaldi mentions is none other than him!

We all will meet up in Singapore and travel together from thereon. La Pérouse had with him a chronometer and other similar gadgets and therefore he could point out the exact location of this mysterious island—Lat. 41° 42' N by Long. 162° 30' W. The island cannot be found on a map. But given its mysterious background, this is only to be expected.

Our journey begins on 25 September.

24 September, Singapore

We have all gathered here since yesterday. I have been listening to Sabatini talk about Christobaldi's document. In the beginning of the manuscript, Christobaldi talks about himself at length. He was a shepherd's son. At the age of thirteen, for the first time, he got an inkling of a future vision. Of course, everyone laughed it off at that time. But soon numerous future events began to appear before him. He learnt to read and write on his own, chiefly to be able to document these occurrences. Just as Nostradamus had, he too proclaimed the exact date and time of his death to others. Christobaldi has mentioned the 1943 great Indian famine. He hasn't mentioned the name of Bengal per se but he has referred to a province of the East. He has also talked about the Second World War, including Hitler's concentration camps.

Suma asked if anything had been written about Japan's future.

Sabatini responded, 'Your King Hirohito is mentioned once. That he will live long is clearly revealed. Apart from this, the Hiroshima and Nagasaki incidents are also marked, as were by Nostradamus.'

I realized Suma was a bit suspicious about this unknown creature we were looking for. He said, 'Humans have accomplished so much in the twentieth century, and I doubt there's any other being that can outdo or even match these achievements.'

But Saunders and Crole are open-minded. Crole said, 'Even if this creature had existed, the first thing I'll look into is whether it could bring the supernatural into the arena of science. Many scientists today scoff at the idea of anything mystical but no one can offer a cogent explanation about this matter.'

Saunders is the most enthusiastic. He is constantly saying, 'Whatever La Pérouse has stated cannot be a lie. He was such a renowned traveller. What we need to work on is if these creatures still exist. What I can't understand is why they keep themselves confined to one island and not communicate with the rest of the world. How can thecommunity continue to remains uperior? To make technological advancements, we require the presence of equipment and other materials. Is it possible all these are available on this one island?'

Of course, we will get no response to such matters sitting in Singapore. But I must confess: I, too, have my suspicions in this matter. There's no dearth of fraud in such affairs. Anyone who can emulate this old style of handwriting, labouring over it for a month, can easily produce a 500-year-old manuscript.

27 September, Pacific Ocean

We started off on 25 September. Suma's vehicle remains matchless. Judging by the directions in La Pérouse's diary, we feel we need to travel over 7500 miles into the ocean. So far we've been covering 500 miles per day. We can go much faster than this but we are inclined to enjoy this trip like a cruise and don't feel the need to hasten. Saunders has brought with him a game called Logos. Five people can play this. It's a game involving the formation of English words. I'd assumed Suma and Sabatini may have problems with it but I can see that despite not being at ease speaking English, they have studied the language well and are equipped with a good vocabulary. We spend a decent amount of time playing the game.

Suma has also brought with him some state-of-the-art electronic gadgets. One of them is really very interesting. It's a translating machine. Suppose you've gone shopping in Paris with no knowledge of French. You give out your list in English. This machine will instantly translate it into French for you.

We have no clear idea how long we will be on this expedition. We are carrying clothes for ten days and have brought plastic tents to sleep in camps and lots of tinned food to eat.

3 October, The Pacific Ocean, 40°6' and 161°30'

We reached the island half an hour ago. We are thrilled that La Pérouse's notes didn't let us down and that there is indeed an island at this latitude and longitude. What a strange island. There's no foliage of any kind, nothing in the name of greenery—it's only sand, stones and dry soil. We haven't come across any living beings other than mosquitoes. Nor have we noticed any insects or reptiles, let alone birds or animals.

We still can't make out the size of the island. I strongly feel that any form of life we find will be much lower down in the civilizational order. There certainly would be signs of a habitat if they were civilized. In whichever direction we look, we haven't spotted a single house.

We all are a bit apprehensive that this whole exercise will end up in a damp squib. Now, it's two in the afternoon. We all feel that we should stay on the island the entire day. We must explore the island too. In the distance we can see higher ground that looks smoother.

Crole and Saunders are organizing our lunch; I too must help out in these tasks. Have to stop writing now.

5 October

Oh, what joy it gives me even to write this. Our mission is a success! One can churn out a book based on our experiences over the last two days. I'll try to capture the events in my diary.

After lunch on the first day, all five of us set out to explore the middle part of the island. The more we walked, the more we realized the ground level was getting higher and smoother. The presence of pebbles and stones was decreasing too. But this smoothness is not natural for such an island. Suma once stopped walking and lay down with his face on the ground, felt it with his hands to test it. He commented, 'Very odd!'

After forty-five minutes of walking, the hill flattened considerable into a plateau and we were able to stop climbing. We realized we had reached the highest point in the island as we could now see the whole circumference of the land mass. After checking out the view, we walked further into the middle of the plateau and noticed a round hole in the ground, measuring about a metre and a half in circumference. We couldn't figure out what was inside it. There was no doubt about its depth because on looking into the hole one could see an impenetrable darkness. Crole is a bit crazy; he took his mouth closer to the hole and let out a loud shout:'Hey ho!'

There was no response; yet it's easy to infer that this hole is not a natural one; the circle is so perfectly round it has got be the creation of a man or human-like creature, although the areas around don't show any signs of habitation.

We have covered four miles. If this hole is the island's centre point, we can tell how large the island is.

We decided to return to camp. We were all excited about the gaping hole but decided to wait till the next day to inspect it further.

It was almost five when we returned to our camp. We all felt tired after such a long walk. We'd already pitched our tents. There were three tents—Crole and Saunders in one, Suma and I in one and the third one was for Sabatini. We got into our respective tents, lay down on plastic sheets and rested for a while. Sabatini alone is facing a problem—he is the only one getting bitten by mosquitoes. He keeps slapping on the unexposed areas of his body every time one of them bites him. He said, 'My blood is of this type. Even in my own country the mosquitoes love sucking my blood.'

At 6.30 in the evening the sun set, and as happens typically in the Pacific Ocean, the island was soon plunged into darkness. I am carrying my own invention—the Luminimax lamps—and when it becomes totally dark these will light up on their own.

Even if these beings are still in existence, when do we get to see them? Won't they turn up for us at all? Do they hold some grudge against us? Are they scared of us?

Fragments of a German song sung in a hoarse voice were filtering out of Crole's tent. Suma admires Western classical music. Just when he was about to insert a cassette containing a Beethoven symphony into the music system, we heard a scream. It was Sabatini.

'Come out and see, come out and see!'

We ran out of our tents and looked towards what Sabatini was pointing at. It was a breathtaking scene.

A stream of green light was beaming into the sky from the plateau we had visited in the afternoon. The same beam that La Pérouse had seen. It definitely looked like a laser beam.

Saunders said, 'It must be coming out of that hole.'

This had struck me too. The source of the light is through this hole.

I couldn't help thinking out aloud. 'I believe these creatures live under the ground,' I said. 'Which is why there's no evidence of their existence outside.'

'But how do we establish any contact with them?' remarked Saunders impatiently.

We noticed that Suma had brought out an instrument from his tent. It looked like a high-tech Japanese invention, resembling a miniature camera. Instead of the lens, however, there was a spout.

Suma spoke normally into the reverse side of the spout, but the volume of his voice had been amplified manifold, reverberating as if coming from the sky. 'If you're familiar with English, please contact us. We are humans. After reading about you we've come here to establish contact with you.'

Within five seconds, a deep metallic voice responded. A voice as mechanical as his can never be human.

'We know you're here. We were waiting to identify your language for communication.'

'We are friends,' said Suma. 'We want to get closer to you. But how do we do so?'

'Come to the origin of the light.'

We hurried towards the beam, curious and excited.

The light faded the moment we came closer to it, to be replaced by a beam of white light. This light too was coming from the hole.

Once again we heard that high-pitched and deep mechanical voice.

'There's a staircase going down the entrance. Please descend one by one. We've organized seating arrangements for all of you.'

Everyone looked in my direction. I guess they wanted me to take the lead. I went closer to the hole. As the light was coming from below, I could clearly see the staircase. I put my foot on the steps and began my descent. The others followed suit.

After fifty metres or so, we arrived at the foot of the staircase. Twenty metres ahead of us we could see a tunnel full of light. After walking through the passage for a couple of minutes we arrived at a circular room. This room too was full of light, though we couldn't figure out the source of the light. There was no lamp in it. In the middle of the room lay a golden table made of unknown metal and surrounding it were five golden chairs. A voice said: 'Sit down. We got this room and furniture made with you in mind.'

The five of us sat down. Once more the voice came to our ears: 'We are seeing humans for the first time. You are just as we imagined. Till now we had heard about you only through gadgets, heard your songs and musical instruments. And now we are actually seeing a real human being.'

'But how come we can't see you,' asked Sabatini. 'We would like to see you. Come closer to us.'

'That cannot happen,' said the voice.

'Why?'

'You won't be able to tolerate our appearance. Ask us what you want to know.'

'Have you arrived from another planet?'

'No.'

'Then?'

'Life was created on earth almost accidentally because of a chemical reaction. We too were created by a similar accident three hundred years ago.'

'But how did you progress so far—despite no direct contact with humans?'

'We had already arrived fully formed. And in the last three hundred years we have progressed further thanks to our own efforts.'

'You mean, you all?'

'Yes. We don't differentiate among each other.'

'How many of you are here?'

'About fifteen thousand. But the number is growing because of a chemical process. There could be thirty thousand of us soon in our underground city.'

'How did you manage to build this city? How did you organize the infrastructure? And how do you put together the materials to conduct all your scientific experiments?'

'We can organize many things with the help of our willpower. When we require anything we collectively wish for it. Through such a practice we get what we desire. If we require any material for a short spell, its durability too is marked for a brief period. For instance, the presence of this staircase. There's no need for one in our life. We have created this through our willpower only for your use. It'll no longer exist after its requirement is over.'

'What exactly is your relationship with nature?' asked Crole.

'There's no relationship. We know how dangerous it is to depend on nature. The world has suffered severe famine due to drought. Just as due to excessive rain there are floods that wash away homes and kill so many humans. In other words, nature has failed human desire and humans have duly suffered. We face no such predicament.'

'What do you do in your spare time? Don't you have your own music, sports or literature?'

'We have no free time. We're constantly looking for ways to progress. Human beings will require another two thousand years to catch up with the level at which we exist.'

Saunders asked, 'What about animals, birds, insects and other forms of life?'

'There's nothing of this kind. We exist solely with our superior knowledge.'

'But there are mosquitoes in your island!' remarked Saunders.

'Mosquitoes? What is that?'

'It's a kind of insect. Don't you know what it is?'

'This is the first time we are hearing about it.'

I thought to myself—in that case why is Sabatini scratching his hands sitting in his chair? I suddenly remembered Sabatini scratching his hands on our journey to the island.On our way here, we had stopped at another island for engine fuel. Have we imported mosquitoes from there?

'What metal is the seat on which we're sitting made of?' askedSuma.

'Gold.'

Amazing! The largest chunk of gold exists in Tutankhamen's bier. But this table is much larger than that.

'Is there any gold mine here?'

'No. We create gold through a chemical process. All our equipment is made of gold. Gold has no value for us. But we know humans value it.'

Sabatini asked excitedly, 'Do you have the formula to create gold?'

'Of course. Otherwise how do we create it?'

Crole said, 'One day we need to return to our country; but no one will believe in our experience. Can't we take one of you with us?Just for a few days? We'll then return him to this place.'

There was a sound of laughter. Then came the voice:'We are not worried about returning. We have always known how to travel without any transport.'

'Then will you allow one of you to accompany us?'

'But we have already said—you won't be able to bear his appearance.'

'Can you alter his appearance? You can accomplish so much and not this?'

There was a brief pause. Then the voice said: 'Give us two days. Goodbye for today. Please return the same way you came.'

Crole protested, 'But we still have questions to ask!'

'What is it?'

'Just as we're known as humans, what are you known as?'

'Your tongue won't be able to utter it.'

'How do we refer to you when we get back to our countries?'

After a gap of two seconds, the reply came: 'Autoplasm'.

'And the name of the city?'

'You can call it Novopolis.'

I too had a few questions. First I asked him, 'Don't you have any illnesses, ailments, diseases here?'

'No.'

'Which means there's no medicine either?'

'No.'

'But how can you say for sure that there will never be any disease? The next time we come here, I'll bring along a few pills of my own invented medicine, Miracurall, and place them on top of this table. In case you fall ill, you're bound get better with it.'

Of course, I was saying this with Christobaldi's prophecy in mind—that humans will find this species and save them from extinction.

We finally left the room. These beings have mastered the art of air conditioning rather well. Because despite the room being underground we thoroughly enjoyed the cool atmosphere. When we arrived near the staircase, we realized it was automated and was now moving upwards.

We returned to our camps in a peculiar state of mind.

Sabatini said, 'We still haven't got proof that they are not humans.'

'That's true,' said Crole.

'They may have fibbed through this whole thing. We couldn't figure out how they're addressing the issue of food. But underground you can artificially grow plants, trees, fruits, flowers.'

'And about the gold?' asked Suma.

Sabatini laughed. 'Do you really think those chairs and table were made of gold?'

'Gold has a special kind of smell,' said Suma. 'I got that from the chairs and the table.'

'What! A smell of gold? I've never heard of such a thing.'

'I know such things,' said Suma with a trace of anger in his voice.

I told them both to calm down. 'It's immaterial whether they are human or not. Since they discovered the laser beam a hundred years ago, one must admit that their knowledge in science is way ahead of ours.'

6 October

Today there's not much we could do about the Autoplasms. We will get to know of their decision tomorrow. We spent our time playing Logos and bathing in the sea. My intuition tells me they are not humans.

As always at dusk, the laser beam came on. We were not expecting any communication from them but soon after the light came on, we heard an announcement in that familiar voice.

'Please come over after half an hour. The same way you did the last time; you'll sit in the same room you sat last time. We'll let you know our decision then.'

After the announcement, Crole said, 'Do you think these are a group of disenchanted scientists, who, not having made a mark in their own country, decided to settle down here?'

'But didn't you see the escalator?' remarked Saunders. 'To build such things one needs various metals, equipment, labour force . . . From where did they get these?'

'Don't forget about their willpower, Saunders,' I said. 'If they really possess such willpower, they can accomplish many things.'

'Well, let's see what they come up with,' said Suma.

7 October

By now, we had a fair idea of when this laser beam switches on. So we started off half an hour early, reaching the central plateau just as the beam lit up. The voice welcomed us and we took the same staircase down to the circular room.

'So have you decided?' asked Crole.

The voice said, 'We'll provide you with one of us. His appearance will be that of a human. He will dress exactly like you. Only his mind will work like that of an Autoplasm.'

'Will he be able to assert his willpower?'

'No. Chiefly because willpower just from one source will yield no result. We used the willpower of fifty Autoplasms in order to build this escalator for you.'

'Then there is no point in staying here for too long,' said Saunders. 'We can leave by the day after tomorrow.'

'Come tomorrow at the same time.'

'Very well.'

9 October

We will leave by 8.30 this morning. Meanwhile, let me quickly recount yesterday's incident.

When we reached the circular room yesterday evening as scheduled, we heard the voice. 'Our representative will reach your camp by using the same path you have used. You can call him Adam, since he is the first human created by us. And do remember one important thing.'

'Yes?'

'How long will it take you to return to your own country from here?'

'We'll reach London in three weeks.'

'Including the day you reach London, Adam will retain his human form for the next seven days. After the end of the seventh day, Adam automatically comes back to us. I assume by then your work with him will be done. Don't stop him from returning. Do remember—he will not be able to exert his own power. Autoplasm is a non-violent creature. Adam is accompanying you unarmed.'

'Suppose our plans get delayed, what then?'

'The result won't be very pleasant. I can't say anything more than this.' We exchanged puzzled looks. The voice spoke again. 'I've noticed that some of you are wearing rings on your fingers. I'm sending five gold rings for each of you through Adam . . . pure gold, 24 carats. I'll feel happy if you accept these.'

I now took out a big bottle containing 1000 Miracurall pills from my pocket and put it on the table. 'Here's the medicine,' I said. 'Hopefully you won't need this. But suppose you do, you need to consume this. You will then understand that humankind is not that backward.'

A little after we returned to camp, we heard footsteps. When we turned to look, we saw a European approaching us.

'Good evening, gentlemen, my name is Adam.'

Sounding surprised, Crole said, 'But you belong to this community?'

'Yes, I'm an Autoplasm.'

'You'll be asked many questions by scientists in our country. Will you be able to answer them?'

'I believe I can.'

'We return tomorrow morning. Tonight you shall sleep in Sabatini's tent.'

'I don't sleep,' said Adam,

'Whatever the case, we set off tomorrow morning. After staying in London for seven days you can return to your own country.'

11 October

Observing him over the last two days, I realize Adam is a very decent fellow. He pays due respect to each of us. However, none of us can match up to Adam's extraordinary capacity in Logos! He played so exceptionally well that we decided to stop playing the game. We're now spending our time chatting with each other and listening to music on Suma's cassette.

Suma has a video camera but he hasn't taken out at all. Though we have an Autoplasm travelling with us, Suma lost interest in taking pictures as the Autoplasm looks no different from any of us.

After giving it due thought, I've arrived at this decision. If they are indeed not humans, and even if they are infinitely superior to us, mankind is much better off with the entire gamut of experiences—joy–grief, dawn–dusk, sun–moon, fruits–flowers, sports–games, animals–birds.

2 November, London

We reached London yesterday. Today at the Royal Albert Hall, in the presence of fifty noted scientists and an audience of 2000, Adam was put to test. It was obvious from the proceedings that he did indeed come from a superior race.

To start with, he told Sweden's renowned mathematician Haans Rudelberg that Auotplasms were familiar with some of Rudelberg's recently published mathematical theories even as far back as seventy years ago. Then Adam placed examples of some more theories that none of our mathematicians had even thought about.

Next, London's biologist, Dr Kincaid got up on the platform and asked Adam, 'It's clear that your science is much advanced, but why are you so keen to prove that you don't belong to humankind? In terms of appearance, I see no difference between you and any human youth. You stated that life was created on its own in your island; how come your appearance is exactly that of humans?'

Adam gently reminded the audience that this was not his real image. 'As humans are unfamiliar with our appearance I've taken the form of a human before coming here.'

This continued for nearly two hours. Professor Mankivitch, Professor Brunius, John Duckworth, Dr Vasilief, Richter Schultz and some such well-reputed physicists, archaeologists, zoologists, mathematicians, botanists from all over Europe admitted defeat in front of Adam. Adam answered all their questions with politeness and humility. Finally, the chairperson of this evening's event, Professor Chartwell, said, 'We are all amazed to encounter this extraordinary person who is much more advanced than Western scientists. And for this we consider ourselves very fortunate. There's no doubt that today will remain a most memorable day in the history of science. But as Mr Adam has not revealed his genuine self in front of us, we will always wonder if he is actually a human being, a man who has reached the pinnacle of science and knowledge.'

The audience in the Royal Albert Hall burst into applause.

We returned to our hotel with Adam. Over the next three days, he has a very busy schedule: a press conference and about three television interviews.

I keep reminding everyone that we have to release him by the evening of 7 November.

Sabatini is staying in another hotel. He asked whether he could take Adam out for dinner on his own. There's no problem in feeding Adam. He has been prepared in such a way that he is easily digesting all human food.

It's been decided that the day after tomorrow, that is on 4 November, after the television interview in the morning, Sabatini will take Adam to his hotel. Sabatini says he requires at least two to three sittings with Adam for research on the article he will write on Autoplasms after his return to Madrid.

4 November

Due to the press conference yesterday, all newspapers have come up with a detailed story on Adam. As his appearance resembles a human, many have raised their doubts about Autoplasms. However, most admitted that the revelation of this amazingly bright young man was indeed a milestone in history.

We are trying our best to protect Adam. Even though Sabatini is very keen to take him away to Madrid, we are not encouraging the idea. After dinner, Adam has to give Sabatini another session. Sabatini said he will drop Adam back to our hotel.

6 November

Crole, Saunders and I are under a lot of stress at present. Yesterday after dinner with Sabatini, Adam never returned to our hotel. None of us had realized that Sabatini was so utterly irresponsible. When we called his hotel this morning we were told that he had left early in the morning. We can't trace him anywhere either. And tomorrow is the seventh. We need to release Adam latest by tomorrow evening. We received a phone call from a newspaper today requesting for a special interview. We had to decline it.

I hope today at some point at least Adam, if not Sabatini, will resurface.

7 November

What a dreadful incident. I'm yet to get over the trauma. After much investigation, Saunders found out that a friend of Sabatini, Professor Alvarez, lives outside London in Sussex. He too is Spanish and teaches Spanish at London University. Saunders believes Sabatini would have taken Adam there.

I said, 'In that case, let's go there right now. It's 3.15 p.m. By 6.30 this evening Adam needs to return to Novopolis.'

Professor Alvarez's house was a two-storeyed affair with a small patch of a garden. It was almost evening when we reached there. When we rang the doorbell, a servant opened the door and on seeing us, instantly said, 'Professor Alavrez is not in town, he has gone to Paris.'

'We are looking for Professor Sabatini,' said Crole.

'He is inside but he is busy now and has asked me not to disturb him.'

'Never mind. We need to meet him urgently.' Saying this, Crole pushed aside the servant and entered the house.

The retainer stood in front of us and retorted, 'You don't have permission to go upstairs.'

'Of course we have.' Crole took out his revolver and pointed it towards the servant.

'But . . . but his room is locked.'

'Where's the room?'

'Upstairs,' blurted out the frightened servant in a quivering voice.

We went to the first floor and saw a locked room on the right. Crole rapped on the door. Once, twice. There was no response. 'Sabatini! Sabatini!' Crole shouted out. Still no answer.

This time Crole went close to the door and said, 'Sabatini, for the last time we're asking you to open the door; otherwise we'll break it open.'

When even this yielded no response, Crole took out his revolver, aimed at the bolt of the door and pulled the trigger. The sound of the shot reverberated in the small hallway. The door opened ajar with a thundering blast and all three of us burst into the room.

What a strange scenario met our eyes. Two chairs were placed facing each other. In one was Sabatini with his back to us, and in the other was Adam all tied up with rope.

Seeing us enter the room, Sabatini looked annoyed. He snarled, 'I was on the verge of learning it and you have spoilt it.'

'What would you have learned?' asked Saunders.

'The formula for making gold!' shouted Sabatini.

'I wouldn't have disclosed it in any case,' said Adam in a determined voice. 'Never, never, never . . .'

Suddenly something strange started happening to him. Within seconds, the handsome Adam transformed into what appeared as a revolting creature with all eyes, all teeth, all nails exposed. It was difficult to imagine such a repulsive being. Sabatini fell from his chair in fright. Crole screamed, 'Mein Gott', and ran away from the room. Only Saunders stayed calm. He remained in the room and said, 'Untie his knots, Shonku.'

I went towards the being that was Adam only a few minutes ago and untied him. The creature turned his large, bloodshot eyes towards Saunders and me and said, 'Thank you.'

The being then stood up on its hairy two legs and said, 'Through telepathy I have been in touch with my fellow beings all this time. Our people have started showing signs of mosquito-related ailments. Had it not been for your medicine, Professor Shonku, no one would have survived. It's time for me to go. Let me now leave.'

With these words, the creature vanished.

I told myself, 'Christobaldi's second prophecy also turned out to be true!'

9

The Tree with Golden Leaves

16 June

Today is my birthday. There's not much to do; it's been drizzling since the morning and I'm sitting in my favourite armchair in my drawing room, staring at the beams on the ceiling, thinking of—oh, so many things. The elderly Newton is all curled up asleep next to my feet. He is now twenty-four years old. A cat normally lives up to the age of fourteen or fifteen, though in some cases one has heard instances of them surviving till twenty. That Newton is alive for these many years is due to the medicine I have invented, Marjarine. The thought that I would be left all alone without Newton pushed me to do some serious research and ten years ago, I discovered this medicine.

I said I was thinking of numerous things but in reality I was thinking of my bygone days—a quite normal activity for people of my age. In fact, it's been a period of reminiscences—just yesterday I was reading the letters my father wrote to me about fifty years ago. Thinking of those letters, my mind had wandered off to the past. For various reasons this gives me such pleasure. There's no doubt that I've tasted success in life. I don't think any other scientist of this country has achieved such international success. My reputation is based chiefly on my inventions and discoveries. In this regard, my place in the scientific firmament is right after Thomas Alva Edison, a fact acknowledged by scientists in all five continents.

I was drawing up a list of my inventions in my mind. Topping the list is Miracurall, a pill which cures all ailments, followed by the Annihilin pistol. In my adventure-oriented life, I have faced perilous situations many times. I needed a weapon for self-defence, yet I cannot tolerate bloodshed. Hence, this pistol, which doesn't just destroy the enemy but simply erases or annihilates him from the scene.

Soon after appeared the air-conditioning pill, which when placed under one's tongue keeps the body warm in winter and cool in summer. Then arrived Remembrain, a tool to revive lost memory. My pill Somnolin is a sure hit for insomnia; Luminimax, an inexpensive devise to create artificial light; Linguagraph, a machine which translates any unknown language into English; Ornithon, to impart lessons to a bird—these are just some of my favourites.

Miracurall was invented during my youth. Many amazing incidents took place in association with this drug which haven't been documented in full detail as I hadn't started maintaining a diary in the early days. Today I shall recount all these incidents, depending of course on my memory; but before I do so I must say a few words about my father.

My father's name is Tripureswar Shonku. He was Giridih's best and only doctor. He followed the Ayurvedic school of natural medicine. People called him Dhanwantari, the physician of the gods. And though he earned well, it was just enough to keep body and soul together; because apart from his regular practice he would treat many poor people free of cost. He would tell me, 'Just because you have the ability doesn't mean you need to earn in profusion. One certainly requires a fair amount of money to lead a comfortable and peaceful life. But that no way means you need to earn in excess. True satisfaction lies in mitigating the suffering of the poor and needy or those who have suffered at the hands of cruel destiny.'

My father's wise words left an indelible impression on my mind.

After clearing my matriculation from Giridih School, I went to Calcutta to study in a college. I myself admit I was a brilliant student. Not only because I always stood first, but because I progressed so rapidly that I finished school at a very young age, a record that remains unbroken even today. I cleared matriculation at twelve; ISC at fourteen;

and I graduated with a BSc with double honours in physics and chemistry at sixteen.

When I returned home to Giridih after clearing my examinations, my father said, 'I feel you are too young to even think of taking up a job. All this while you have concentrated on science. Now for the next four years, I suggest you look at a different subject. Art, literature, history, philosophy—is there any dearth of subjects? If you can't find suitable books here, you just let me know and I'll get them from Calcutta for you.' After a thoughtful pause, he said, 'I wouldn't at all mind if you devoted your entire life to research instead of doing a regular job. You're my only child. After I die a part of my savings will go for public welfare; the rest will come to you. Hence . . .'

I interrupted him and said, 'No, Baba. I'll devote myself for the next four years studying various disciplines but after this I have to fend for myself. I'll not attain any peace of mind till I stand on my own two feet.'

Baba said, 'Very well. But whichever way you choose to earn your living, don't ever forget compassion and don't ever be indifferent to people who are deprived, illiterate, unable to stand on their own feet resolutely with their head firmly placed over their shoulders.'

Thus at the age of twenty, after four years of studying various other disciplines, I found a job as a lecturer in physics at Scottish Church College. Quite a few of my students were my age; some were even older! But I was never disrespected or taunted or teased by my students. Primarily because even at that young age, I had naturally acquired a quiet personality.

I stayed in rented accommodation and would return home during the summer and autumn breaks. Two-and-a-half years after I started working, I returned home for the summer break. I handed over my luggage to our retainer and went inside my father's room—I was so shocked at the sight that met my eyes that I forgot to breathe. My father lay flat on the floor next to his desk.

In one leap, I reached him and bent down to check on his pulse; I realized he had only lost consciousness. I immediately called for Dr Sarbadhikari.

Baba got back to his senses before the doctor arrived. I helped him get up from the floor and lie down on his bed. Seeing my father indisposed left me with a strange feeling—I had never seen him so weak and helpless before. He saw my worried look and smiled. 'This isn't the first time, my dear Tilu, I've faced this twice before but I have never told you.'

'Why does this happen, Baba?'

'The heart stops to function suddenly. There's no treatment for this. One fine day I'll suddenly leave you due to this.'

Later I came to know my father's ailment is called a heart block. That people no longer die of this is thanks to the invention of pacemaker that runs on battery and keeps the heartbeat regular. It is inserted inside the chest near the heart through surgery.

Nearly two years later, I again went home for the autumn break. This time too Baba looked extremely weak and unwell. On the day of my arrival, however, my father recounted an amazing tale to me.

After dinner, when we both were sitting in the drawing room, my father said suddenly, 'Have you heard of Tikribaba?'

I nodded. 'The person who meditates sitting under a banyan tree in a village on the other side of the Usri River?'

'Yes. He has earned quite a reputation here. A lot of people go to pay him a visit. The day before yesterday, a few of his followers brought this Tikribaba to my house. From what I could gather, he was suffering from breathing trouble and they asked if I could help him with some medication. I was busy giving instructions about his medicine to his followers when suddenly Baba pointed out in a mix of Hindi and Bengali, "You're busy treating me but what about your own ailment?" I've no idea how he came to know about my illness. In any case, I explained to him that my illness has no treatment. "Of course, there must be," he said loudly despite his asthmatic spasms. "Have you heard of *Swarnaparnee*?"

'I realized he was referring to a golden tree. Not a tree but a herb. It is mentioned in the ancient Sanskrit book of Ayurvedic medicine, the *Charak Samhita*, but in contemporary times no one has found any trace of this herb. When I told Babaji as much, he said, "I know where this tree is. In my youth when I was living in Kashi, I suffered from a severe case of jaundice. My guru had a few leaves of Sonepatti. He turned two dry leaves into powder, mixed it in milk and gave it to me to drink. Before going to bed, I drank it in one gulp and lo and behold . . . in the morning, the jaundice had vanished. What a relief it was! I know where you can get leaves of the tree. You have to travel to Kasauli in Himachal Pradesh. About nine kilometres to the north of this town there are some ruins of an old Chamunda temple. There's a forest behind this temple and there's a waterfall in that forest. And beside this waterfall grows this Swarnaparnee tree. Only this medicine can cure you. No other treatment will."'

My father sighed. 'There was a time when I would have gone to any length to hunt for trees and herbs. But now it's too late.'

Meanwhile, I had already made up my mind. I said, 'Because you're unable to go does not mean that I can't go either? Tomorrow, I shall start my journey to Kasauli. You never know—Babaji's words may well turn out to be true. And more so since you say that Swarnaparnee is mentioned in the *Charak Samhita* . . .'

Shaking his head gently, my father smiled and said, 'No, Tilu, no need to go right now. You need to reach Kasauli from Kalka . . . it's quite a long distance. By the time you return it'll be at least five to seven days. And by then you may find I'm no more. Please don't go now.'

After two days, my father passed away from a blockage of the heart. Even though I couldn't use this to cure my father I'd decided that I would visit Kasauli to hunt for the Swarnaparnee. Two weeks of holidays were still left after the completion of my father's last rites. Without wasting any more time. I set off for Kasauli. It took me two-and-a-half days to reach Kalka from Giridih.

My heart was rather heavy due to my father's untimely death but felt much lighter after reaching this quiet picturesque town in the foothills. This small town is 46 kilometres from Kalka at an altitude of 6500 feet in Himachal Pradesh. You need to reach here in a taxi from Kalka. Its clean fresh air makes it a health resort.

After checking into an inexpensive hotel, without wasting any further time, I straightaway went to the manager, Nandkishore Rawal, and asked him if he had heard of the Chamunda temple. 'Of course I have,' responded the manager. 'But to reach there you need to use a horse.'

I also asked if there was a forest behind the temple. 'Yes, there is,' Nandkishore said. 'A very deep, dense forest.'

Nandkishore himself arranged for a horse for me. This was my first experience at horse riding but I soon realized riding wasn't a problem; in fact I was quite enjoying it. I was accompanied by the owner of the horse, Chhotelal, who was astride his own mount. After reaching the temple ruins, I dismounted and told Chhotelal, 'I am going into the forest. I'm looking for a tree. You may have to wait for a couple of hours.'

'Please don't go alone, Babuji,' begged Chhotelal. 'There are tigers and leopards and other wild creatures in the jungle.'

'Would you like to come along?' I asked him.

'Yes, Babuji.'

After tying up the two horses to some trees, we entered the forest. When Chhotelal asked me what I was looking for, I told him the story about Swarnaparnee. Chhotelal said he had never heard of this tree.

After fifteen minutes of trekking, we heard the bubbling sound of a stream. Soon we reached the waterfall. It was dark because of the dense foliage, except for one spot where the sunrays had managed to push through the gaps in the leaves and were shining like a theatre spotlight on a gleaming, waist-high shrub adorned with yellow leaves. There was no doubt in our minds that this was Swarnaparnee.

My heart danced with joy. I hadn't expected my mission would be such a success in such a short time. But I could see only one tree. Would I find some more if I went further? Chhotelal and I went in different directions looking for more Swarnaparnee bushes. When we couldn't locate any more Swarnaparnee trees after fifteen minutes of searching, we returned to the waterfall. I'd already decided what I would do if I found the tree. In a jute bag I was carrying a spade I'd bought in Kasauli. I was going to dig the tree out by the roots and take it back with me to Giridih.

After watching me use the spade ineffectually, Chhotelal remarked, 'Ram! Ram!' and snatched away the spade from my amateur hands. Within five minutes, he had uprooted the tree and handed it over to me. Three days later, as soon as I returned to Giridih, the first thing I did was to call for my gardener, Harkishan. I showed him the herb and asked him, 'Have you seen this stuff before?'

Shaking his head, Harkishan said with a frown, 'Never, never.'

Harkishan caressed the yellow leaves with his hands and asked if it produced any medicine. I said, 'Yes, excellent medicine.'

'Then just one tree will be of no use, Babuji.'

I looked at him. 'Can you arrange for some more trees to be produced from this one?'

The gardener said, 'If we graft it to other trees, or plant a particular part of a branch in the ground, another tree may appear.'

'Then please do whatever you can,' I said.

I now decided to test its potential. If Tikribaba's directions for finding the tree were correct, one could infer that the cure for jaundice would also be correct.

Before leaving Giridih, I had heard that our local lawyer, Joygopal Mitra, was grievously ill. He used to be my father's patient. I address his wife as mashima or aunt. I spoke to her on the phone and was told Mitra Babu was suffering from ascites. 'I can see doomsday, Tilu!' wailed Jayanti mashima. 'All doctors have given up.'

When I broached the topic of Swarnaparnee, she heaved a sigh and said, 'So many drugs were used on him, what harm will yet another one do?' I could feel that she wasn't too hopeful.

I reached Mitra Babu's residence along with two crushed Swarnaparnee leaves in a paper sachet. I handed it over to the lawyer's wife. 'Give this to him after mixing it in half a cup of milk, mashima. I'll come to see you tomorrow morning.'

I could hardly sleep the night due to anxiety.

When in the morning I sat in my drawing room and Dukhi had just placed a cup of tea in front of me on the table, the phone rang. I leapt to the phone and said 'hello'. I was greeted with Jayanti mashima's loud scream, 'TILU!' she shrieked so loudly that I had to move the receiver a few inches away from my ear. 'Tilu, baba Tilu! Come and see, your uncle has returned from hell!'

I hadn't as yet decided what I would do with the medicine if it worked, but the news of Mitra Babu's recovery and the miracle drug spread fast, and far and wide in Giridih. So I didn't have a choice but to attend to a few incurable ailments. Needless to say, in each case, my medicine worked. I've always been asked where I acquired this amazing drug but I've always had to lie: I always say that before dying my father had given me the drug and that I was clueless of both its name and its provenance. In the meantime, thanks to my gardener's perseverance and his strategy in planting all the new bushes facing the southern wall of my garden, eleven Swarnaparnee trees took root and started flourishing. I assumed each one would produce fresh leaves each year and there would thus be no shortage of the medicine.

If I've given you the idea that I had completely given up on my academic pursuit in Calcutta and had devoted myself to the medical profession, I ought to set right this scenario. My teaching in Calcutta was on in full swing. No one was as yet aware of Swarnaparnee in Calcutta because I had not spoken about it to anyone. However, I decided to keep some leaves with me in case I heard of someone known to me to be in the clutches of death.

I wasn't too happy with this traditional method of mixing the powder of the leaves in milk. So I decided to create Swarnaparnee pills. Within a month, my mission turned into a reality. On my twenty-fifth birthday, while on summer vacation in Giridih, I was turning the handle of a machine and the tube attached to it was producing pill after pill which were gathering inside a bowl. Right then, in a flash, a name for this pill came to my mind—Miracurall. That is, miracle to cure all complaints. A pill to destroy all illnesses.

At this very time, an incident took place which became a turning point of my life.

I was in Calcutta at that point. Within a few months of taking up my job as lecturer, I had decided to subscribe to the renowned science-based English journal, *Nature*. One day, soon after my discovery of Miracurall, I read an excellent article on biology. It was written by someone called Jeremy

Saunders. According to the list of contributors in the journal, Saunders had graduated in biology from Cambridge two years back. One could deduce he was about my age. I wrote a letter to Jeremy Saunders, at his London residence. In those days, it took eighteen days for a letter to reach London via ship and eight days via plane. I sent the letter by airmail. I received a reply from Saunders after nineteen days. That is, he too replied by airmail. He was not just delighted to receive my letter but also, through my letter, he said he found the voice of a gifted and intelligent fellow scientist. In the last few lines of the letter, he mentioned that he was born in the city of Poona in India. 'My grandfather was part of the British Indian Army for thirty-two years. I came over to England with my parents at the age of seven; but the memories of India of that seven-year-old and my love and affection for India and Indians are still fresh.'

Our correspondence continued. In his third letter, Saunders wrote, 'Though we both are twenty-five now, I don't believe that we can't become penfriends at this age. I shall wait to get your consent on this.'

Naturally I agreed to Saunders's offer. We exchanged each other's photographs and continued to write regularly to each other.

After eight months of this monthly correspondence, there was a gap of a month with no reply from Saunders.

I decided to send a telegram after waiting for another two weeks. I know Saunders didn't have a regular job. He was still doing his research in life science.

On the seventh day, an airmail letter arrived from London. The handwriting on the envelope wasn't Saunders's. It looked very feminine. While opening the envelope I remembered Saunders had said he had got married last year and that his wife's name was Dorothy. Yes, the letter was indeed from Dorothy.

But such an unfortunate piece of news! 'I can't tell you what state I'm in to inform you of this,' wrote Dorothy. 'Because you're such a close friend of Jerry, this duty becomes even more difficult.' After this preamble a thunder-strike. 'Cancer has been detected in Jerry's liver. According to doctors, he can survive for only another two months.'

The moment I read this, I decided on my plan of action. I put ten Miracurall pills in an envelope and addressed it to Dorothy, and sent it by immediate airmail. In the letter I enclosed with the pills, I made an earnest request. 'The minute you receive this parcel please give two pills to your husband. If there's no improvement in the first two days, give him two more. If need be please give all ten pills. The instant you feel it's working, please send me a telegram.'

Days passed with no news from London. I waited a month—no news. Saunders had my addresses in both Giridih and Calcutta. Still no news. I feared the worst. Did that mean Miracurall doesn't work with cancer? In that case, I ought to change its name!

A month and a half later, I was back in Giridih for the autumn break. A day before Diwali I'd drafted a telegram to Dorothy and was rereading it in a very saddened state before sending it when Dukhi appeared, excited. 'A Sahib is alighting from a taxi.'

I heard the doorbell ring. The first room in my house is the drawing room. When I opened the door, I saw a handsome, golden-haired European standing before me, sporting a wide smile. Thanks to the exchange of our photographs, we were familiar with each other's faces. Hence, without any hesitation, I embraced Saunders and in a choked voice blurted, 'You're alive!'

By now, we were both inside the room and Dukhi had taken away his suitcase. Saunders slapped me on the shoulders, dropped on the sofa and remarked, 'That you can jolly well see for yourself. But tell me frankly—is this an Indian trick? This has created an uproar in the medical fraternity in London. What tablet did you send me?'

After asking Dukhi to make us coffee I recounted the entire story of the Swarnaparnee. Saunders said in an offended tone, 'All this time you have kept such an incident from this penfriend of yours?'

I spoke the truth. 'I was afraid that you may not be convinced by it which may result in an estrangement between us.'

'Nonsense. What reflects very clearly in your letters are your lucid thoughts and the profundity. How can I not believe in your findings? What's the name of this remarkable medicine?'

'I've already disclosed the Sanskrit word to you; and the name which I've coined is Miracurall.'

'Bravo!' yelled Saunders. 'Nothing can be nicer! But I hope you've taken the patent on this drug?'

When I said 'no', Saunders leapt up from the sofa. 'Are you mad? Don't you realize this medicine will turn you into a millionaire?'

With a sardonic smile I said, 'That's exactly what I want to avoid. I've no attraction for wealth. As long as I can lead a life with basic comforts I'm happy.'

Saunders slapped his hand on the arm of the sofa and said, 'Damn it, Shonku! You may win a Nobel Prize for this, do you know?'

'No, Saunders; I can't. You just heard, all I've done regarding this medicine is to locate this tree. That too was possible as I was given the direction by someone. And its virtues are nature's contribution. Whom will you confer the prize on?'

'Very well, let's forget about the prize; but there's something in the name of reputation! Are you indifferent to this too? After all, you can't deny that it's only you who is in possession of Miracurall. As this cures cancer, you can imagine its true potential. You're the sole copyright holder of this most powerful drug. Won't people across the world want to know you?'

'But what do you want me to do?'

'I propose this—come along with me to London. The news of my miracle cure created a real stir not just within the medical profession but even amongst the scientific fraternity. They want to see you; they want to hear all about this medicine straight from you; and more importantly, what they are very curious to find out are the components of this drug—what does it contain so powerful and so strong which combats all diseases. Have you done its chemical analysis?'

'No.'

'In that case we'll do it in London. Once its ingredients get identified one can produce it artificially to release it in the market. You can imagine what confidence it can instil in an individual's mind. Therefore, I request you to come to London with me. I'm sure you agree that the main centre for modern science is now in the West. Don't you want to go in person as a scientist to England?'

Saunders's proposal was too tempting to refuse. To be frank, I'd long nursed a desire to visit England, but I didn't realize it would become a reality so soon.

I went to Calcutta to organize my trip.

On 25 October 1937, Saunders and I set off from Bombay to England in P&O Company's ship, SS *Athena*. On 16 November, we alighted from the ship at Portsmouth and took a train to London's Victoria Station. From there we took the Underground to reach Hampstead. Saunders lives in Hampstead, on Willoughby Road.

Through Saunders's letters I knew that his parents also lived with him and his wife. His father, Jonathan Saunders, taught history in London University.

Seeing us, everyone's face lit up with smiles and they all greeted me with warmth and affection. Saunders's mother embraced me and said, 'You've saved Jerry from the jaws of death; we can never pay you back.'

The Saunderses lived in a two-storeyed house. I was given a room on the ground floor.

At dinner that evening, Saunders discussed his plans.

'Tomorrow morning we'll organize the chemical analysis of your pill. Thereafter, we need to fix a venue for your lecture and put up an advertisement in the papers for the general public. Of course, I'll separately call up all scientists and doctors whom I know personally to let them know.'

'What will you announce in the advertisement?' I asked. 'No one here knows me by my name.'

Without any hesitation, Saunders responded, 'I'll say, "The destroyer of all diseases, the inventor of this revolutionary drug, Miracurall, the Indian scientist Professor T. Shonku will deliver a lecture on his invention." How does that sound?'

I said, 'Oh no! I'll never be able to promote myself as an inventor. That would amount to lying.'

Saunders scolded me. 'Why do you say you're not an inventor? Who traced the tree—a tree that has been mentioned only in an ancient Sanskrit medicinal treatise, that other than a Kashi-based holy man no one else has seen or heard of? Who undertook the perilous journey on a horse at a height of 6500 feet, entering a deep and dense forest, risking his life? You or anyone else? You're so intelligent and sagacious; don't you understand that it was you who "discovered" this tree and put it to its rightful use?'

What could I say after this? The elder Saunders said, 'Have your food, Shonku. Don't sit back with your head bent. What Jerry has said is 100 per cent the truth. To earn one's rightful due is the sure sign of a wise man. This is not the time to be humble and modest.'

The next morning, after breakfast, Saunders told me he was going into town to meet with other scientists. 'Today, I'll not drag you with me; why don't you take a walk with Dorothy in Hampstead Heath and get some fresh air? You can also look out for Keats's house which is a ten-minute walk from here.'

I'd heard of Hampstead Heath. This is a wide expanse of grassland. After seeing everyone else off, Dorothy and I went for a walk. I wrapped up as it was November and rather cold, much colder than Giridih in winter.

Dorothy is a very intelligent woman; I could gather that after talking to her for only five minutes. She had met Jeremy while she was studying economics at Cambridge. I knew through newspaper reports about the rise of Hitler and the all-powerful Nazi party apparatus in Germany. But in India I had hardly realized the ferocity of the level of Hitler's megalomania and the Nazi terror that he had let loose. Dorothy said, 'You know, there's something called "mad after power" in English. Hitler is mad in that sense. He is dreaming and planning to grab the entire European mainland and turn it into a greater Germany or what they fashionably call the Lebensraum.'

Seeing me turning grim, Dorothy said, 'Just look at me! This is your first trip to London and I'm upsetting you with such bleak thoughts. Very sorry, Shonku. Now let's go over to see Keats's house, which I'm sure will cheer you up.'

Dorothy wasn't wrong. I marvelled at the upkeep of their Poet Laureate John Keats's house. I can't think of history and memories of a significant personality in our country being preserved and kept alive with such care. Dorothy said, 'This is not just Britain's speciality; wherever you go in Europe you'll find such similar things.'

Saunders returned at 6.30 in the evening. The first thing he said was, 'Your lecture has been organized at Caxton Hall for the day after tomorrow at 7 p.m. The announcement will come out in *The Times* and the *Manchester Guardian*. I've informed many people via telephone, like my doctor who treated me for my cancer—Dr Cunningham—he too will be there. Everyone is eagerly waiting to hear you.'

'And what news of my pill's analysis?'

Saunders took out an envelope from his pocket and gave it to me. It carried the analysis report. I glanced over it and remarked, 'Well, I can see the presence of all kinds of vitamins. Apart from that there's potassium, calcium, phosphorus, iron, iodine . . . this looks like you're going through all the components of garlic.'

Saunders said, 'It's the presence of allyl sulphide that kills so many germs.'

'But what's mentioned at the end of this report is significant. It says there's one ingredient in this pill which cannot be identified chemically.'

'Exactly,' said Saunders. 'And because of this it can't be produced in a lab artificially. Or in other words, Shonku, you're the sole proprietor of this medicine. No one can take your place.'

This statement left me with mixed feelings. It doesn't feel bad to admit that Miracurall belongs to me alone; yet it's also true that because this drug can't be reproduced and released in the market, millions of dying people will be deprived of this life-saving medicine.

The next day I went out with Saunders and visited many of London's well-known spots—the British Museum, National Gallery, Madame Tussauds. In the evening at the Mermaid Theatre we saw Bernard Shaw's play *Pygmalion*. In all I could say that London hadn't disappointed me.

I could never imagine that there would be such a crowd for my lecture. Saunders came along with me to the dais, stood in front of the microphone and introduced me. Saunders's teacher, Raymond Carruthers, chaired the meeting. Saunders had already coached him. After he spoke a few words about 'a brilliant young Indian scientist Professor Shonku', it was my turn to speak.

As I had been teaching students for years, I faced no inhibition in delivering a lecture in public. Hence, with ease, I spoke about India's Ayurvedic system, the *Charak Samhita* and *Sushruta Samhita*, about my father, and how, after hearing Tikribaba's directions, I went in search of Swarnaparnee in Kasauli's forest. There was pin-drop silence in the hall. Judging by the applause that I received after my lecture, I felt I had passed a test.

Following my lecture, a time slot was allotted for a Q&A session. I'd answered the two most obvious questions in my lecture: one, if I would market my drug, and two, if I would practise for a while in London. Therefore, after waiting for a couple of minutes, Saunders escorted me off the dais. After shaking hands with many people, and replying 'Thank you' in response to at least fifty congratulations, I found myself free.

The next day I saw all the papers in London carrying reports of my lecture along with my photograph.

Seeing my bewildered state, Saunders remarked, 'There's no need to be so surprised, Shonku. There were a lot of reporters present at Caxton Hall. You forget that nothing as exciting as the invention of Miracurall has occurred in the recent past. No paper could be indifferent to you and your Swarnaparnee.'

In London, Saturday and Sunday are holidays. Very few stay back in London on these two days; they go to the countryside in England to spend two peaceful days. Saunders had already informed me that he would take me to Oxford and Cambridge over the weekend—Cambridge on Saturday for the night and Oxford the next day. Dorothy also accompanied us.

I was overwhelmed to see these two renowned old universities. It's difficult to decide which one is better, though as a city the quiet beauty of Cambridge wins hands down over Oxford. Both Saunders and Dorothy had passed out from King's College. I feel there isn't a better atmosphere for pursuing education.

On Sunday when we returned home at 4.30 p.m. and entered the main door, Saunders's mother rushed towards us.

'A young foreigner is waiting to see Shonku for half an hour.'

'What do you mean by "foreigner"', asked Saunders.

'Once you meet him you will understand. All I can say is he is unable to speak English like us.'

When we entered the drawing room, a young lad, wearing glasses and sporting thick golden hair, got up from the sofa.

'Guten . . . er, good evening,' said the lad. I could gather the fellow was either German or Austrian; he had stopped himself from uttering *Guten abend* and said good evening in English. Let me mention here that while I was doing nothing for four years after my graduation, I learnt German and French with the help of Linguaphone records on the gramophone.

Dorothy didn't join us. After the three of us settled down, the youth apologized for his English.

'My name is Norbert Steiner,' said that boy. 'I live in Berlin; I've come from there.'

Then he looked straight at me and said, 'The news about Miracurall has appeared in our papers and everyone is discussing this. I've come to meet you in connection with this amazing drug. I called up Caxton Hall where you'd delivered your lecture and found out that you were staying at Hampstead. After reaching here I checked with a drug store that Mr Saunders lives in Willoughby Road.'

'May I know the reason for your visit?' asked Saunders.

'Before this I want to pose two questions.'

'Yes?'

'You know that the Nazis are committing horrible torture on the Jews, don't you?'

I'd read about this in my own country. Hitler thinks the Jews have been harming Germany in various capacities for a very long time and that they should be eliminated from Germany for that country to get back its former glory. According to Hitler, Jews are not even human: and the real Germans were those whose veins do not carry even a drop of Jewish blood. With this excuse, he was carrying out heinous crimes on them. Even German Jewish intellectuals, many of those who occupied top positions in the country, were being targeted.

Saunders said, 'Yes, I do. What's your second question?'

'Have you heard of Heinrich Steiner?'

'Heinrich Steiner? I know the name,' said I. 'He teaches Sanskrit, doesn't he? And has translated the Vedas and Upanishads into German?'

'Yes,' said Norbert Steiner. 'I'm referring to him.'

'How do you know him?'

'He is my father. He was a Sanskrit teacher in a German University. The Nazis have thrown out the Jews from all universities. Have you heard of the Gestapo?'

'I'm familiar with that word, too,' I said, 'Germany's secret state police?'

'Yes. The second most powerful person in Germany after Hitler is Hermann Göring. It is he who has created the Gestapo. Each person in this police force is a devil. Nothing stops them from committing any evil deed.'

'Is your father—?'

'Yes. He has been assaulted mercilessly. For some time my father was toying with the idea of leaving Germany; but he was in a dilemma since Berlin is his place of birth. He is respected and loved by his students and didn't want to leave. Two days ago, armed Gestapo police arrived at our house. This was in the afternoon. We had just started our lunch. One police aimed a pistol at my father and said, "Repeat—Heil Hitler".

I had also heard about the salute made by Germans devoted to Hitler, extending the right arm and shouting 'Heil Hitler'. It won't be too wrong to translate this as 'Hitler Zindabad'.

Norbert continued, 'Despite repeated orders, my father refused to say 'Heil Hitler'. Then the police attacked him. After beating him up, they left, with my father lying on the floor, half-dead. His entire body was smeared in blood, and he had a fractured skull. No Jews are allowed inside any German hospitals. Our family physician, Dr Hubermann, who is also Jewish, never leaves his house nowadays. My sister and I nursed him as best as we could. But the state he is at present—delirious, with very high fever—I don't think he can survive beyond a few days. In yesterday's paper I read about Professor Shonku and Miracurall.'

Norbert's distressed look now turned towards me.

'If you can save my father . . .'

Saunders said, 'Do you want to take the professor to Berlin?'

The boy nodded. 'Yes. Otherwise, I think, my father won't survive, Mr Saunders. My father is a genuine admirer of India. He has been to India seven times. He says that no other language can offer the wealth that Sanskrit can. I'm carrying some money. Tomorrow afternoon at 11.30 a plane will leave from Heston and reach Berlin at 4.30 p.m.

The professor will stay with us in our house. In two days' time I'll put him back on a plane. He won't need to spend any money.'

'But how will you arrange for his safety?'

'The Nazis have nothing against Indians,' said Norbert. 'I can assure you that no harm will come to him.'

Saunders paused for a brief spell and then said, 'Can your father be identified as a Jew?'

'Yes, he can.'

'Is his hair black?'

'Yes.'

'Then how come your hair is golden? Is your mother's hair like yours?'

'No, my mother too had black hair. She died five years ago.'

Norbert now tugged at his hair and the golden wig came off to expose his black hair.

'Now you know how I can roam around so freely. In addition, Steiner is not strictly a Jewish name; it can belong to others too. I can assure you, Dr Shonku will face no danger.'

I was thinking . . . had my father been alive he would have surely said, 'Please go, Tilu. Your life will be blessed if you can save a learned man's life.'

Saunders looked very worried at the thought of my going to Berlin at this time. He now turned towards me and said, 'What's your take on this, Shonku?'

I said, 'If I can save such an esteemed Indologist from death's door my soul will rest in peace.'

'Then please go,' said Saunders, 'but please don't stay beyond two days. I'm also telling you, Norbert ... if by God's grace and thanks to Miracurall your father recovers, please don't announce it publicly. Otherwise, Shonku will have to stay back in Berlin indefinitely to treat at least a dozen dying patients.'

'I promise such a thing will not happen.'

Norbert got up and said, 'Tomorrow morning at 10 I'll reach here in a taxi.'

After Norbert left, Saunders asked me, 'How many Miracurall pills are you carrying with you?'

'Twenty-four.'

'Where have you kept these?'

'In a bottle inside my suitcase. For immediate treatment I always carry four pills on my person. But in Berlin I'll carry all my pills. Four will be in my pocket and the rest in my bag.'

'What I fear is that the news of your miracle medicine has already reached Germany; suppose you fall into a Nazi trap? Many may be suffering from incurable diseases. My blood curdles just to think of some of them exploiting your medicine.'

'Not to worry, Saunders. It's not so easy to identify an individual only through a newspaper photo. Also, there are many Indians of my age who are studying there.

Believe you me, no one will figure me out as the Shonku of Miracurall fame.'

Saunders heaved a sigh and said, 'That's fine; but do remember that till you return I will not relax.'

Saunders was writing an article for a zoology-based journal, so he shooed us out of the house. 'I need some peace and quiet so you and Dorothy go out for a walk.'

We had no particular place to visit. Dorothy and I walked around Hampstead before stopping at a small cafe. While we were waiting for our coffee, Dorothy said, 'I've developed such an adverse reaction to Germany and the German race that every time I hear someone go there my first reaction is always to stop that person from doing so. Of course, I do understand your case. It's very natural for you to develop such respect for Heinrich Steiner.'

I said, 'A lot of Germans have deep respect for Indian art and literature. And this is not a contemporary interest. It goes back to over two hundred years. Our noted ancient Sanskrit play *Shankuntala* was translated into German in the early nineteenth century.'

'At that time the midday sun was shining on Germany, Shonku. Now that country has plunged into darkness; people are all blind; with the result they can't see the real personality of Hitler.'

That evening, I went to my room to pack after dinner and coffee. Just when I'd lifted the suitcase on my bed I heard a knock on my door. Saunders was at the door.

'May I come in?'

'Of course.'

After entering, Saunders shut the door and raised an unexpected question.

'Are you familiar with firearms?'

'Are you referring to a pistol or gun?'

'Yes.'

I had to admit that I'd no experience in this. 'To be frank I was rather good with the catapult at the age of eight or ten. Normally at such an age, boys are adept in killing birds with it and brag about it. But I never killed anyone with it. Since my childhood I could not put up with any bloodshed.'

'I'm also like that, Shonku,' said Saunders. 'But I swear I won't hesitate to shoot those who commit inhuman atrocities on innocent souls. The Bible proclaims: If someone slaps you on one cheek, turn to them the other also . . . I do not subscribe to this.'

'But why are you telling me this?'

Saunders put his hand inside his pocket and took out a revolver. 'This is made in Germany. It's called a Luger automatic. I've inserted six bullets in it. Please take this with you to Berlin. Study it now. This is the safety catch. Only when you press it can the trigger be squeezed. It's not right to assume that just because your aim at catapult was good you will be proficient in the use of a revolver. In fact, instead of a revolver, it's much easier to aim through a rifle. If you aim a revolver at someone at a point-blank range, you can definitely injure him to an extent. Therefore, please extend your hand.'

I reluctantly took the revolver. Even though I was lean and thin and stood 5'7" tall, I was full of energy. This is thanks to my father, who advocated consuming nutritious food and daily exercise—a dictum I follow to this day.

Nowadays all big jet planes fly 30,000 to-35,000 feet above ground level. With the result that if you look down from your window in the plane, you see almost nothing. The plane in which I was travelling to Berlin with Norbert had four propellers and as it was flying low because of the short distance we were travelling, I could clearly see houses, roads and farmlands. How serene and charming are these scenes. As this was winter, the greenery was limited and on occasion I saw snow-filled fields as well.

We landed at Berlin airport late in the afternoon. In those days, the word 'airport' was not yet popular. One referred to it as aerodrome. It was much smaller by today's standards but even then one had to go through various rules and regulations.

We had to wait in line to be cleared by a rotund German sitting behind a counter, checking everyone's passports. When my turn came, I handed my passport to the official. In addition, I had to give a yellow card in which I'd mentioned personal details like country of origin, expected length stay in Germany and the reason of my coming here. I'd filled up these details en route in the plane.

The inspector kept glancing at me as he leafed through my passport. Then in a measured tone, he whispered my name 'Shonku' three times in the form of a question, '*Arzt?*' He was asking me if I was a doctor. I said, '*Nein, Wissenschaftler. Professor.*' No, I'm a scientist. A professor.

Now the fellow turned towards a uniformed policeman standing behind him and asked, '*Fritz, anerkennen sie das herr?*' Do you recognize this gentleman?

'Nein, Nein,' came the reply. No, no.

'For how long will you stay here?' the inspector asked, turning towards me.

I said, 'Around three days.'

'The reason for this visit?'

'To travel. It's mentioned in the card.'

'Very well. Go ahead.'

Well! I had crossed one hurdle. It looked like this gentleman had read about me in the newspaper and found a marked resemblance between the photographs in my passport and the newspaper article.

As we exited the aerodrome after collecting my luggage, I observed a few people looking at me with curiosity. I won't deny it left me feeling rather uncomfortable.

After getting into a cab, Norbert gave the direction to the driver, 'Number 17 *Friedrichstrasse.*'

It took me no time to realize that Berlin was the world's third largest city. I also realized the city seemed to run on clockwork precision; there was a certain discipline in the movements of the people here. The character of this city bore no resemblance with London at all. The number of Indians I saw on the streets of London was far more than in Berlin, though I knew many Indians were either studying or working here.

After half an hour, Norbert asked the driver stop on the right. The taxi stopped in front of a double-storeyed house.

After settling the fare with the driver, Norbert picked up our suitcases and went to the main door and pressed the doorbell. Soon, a retainer opened the door and relieved him of the luggage. Norbert hurriedly led me up the stairs to the second floor.

'You'll check on my father first, right?' he asked.

'Yes, right away.'

We walked through a book-lined room to enter a bedroom. On one side of the room in a bed was an elderly figure lying under a quilt, his eyes shut. There was some grey hair along with his thinning black hair, and he looked to be in his mid-fifties. The bandages on his head and elbow had obviously been done by an amateur, most probably somebody in the family as the doctor was unable to visit the patient. The man was clearly in stress, breathing heavily and wheezing. It was Heinrich Steiner.

Standing next to the bed stood a young girl of about sixteen, wiping away her tears. Norbert pointed at her and said, 'My sister, Leny.'

I went forward and checked the patient's pulse. It was faint and nearly non-existent. I was beside my father when he was on his deathbed. The shadow of death I had seen on his face was palpable on Heinrich Steiner's face too.

There was no time to waste.

I realized he was in no position to take the medicine by himself. I'd already crushed two of my pills and brought them along with me. I told Leny, 'Right next to you I see a flask and glass on a table. Pass me a glass of water.'

While Leny was pouring out the water, a sound made me look at Professor Steiner's direction. His lips were quivering. A sound came out. 'A-ha.' I looked at Norbert.

'My mother's name was Hanna.'

The professor's mouth was still wide open. I poured the powdered tablets into the glass of water and slowly made the sick man drink the potion.

'Is there anything else to be done?' asked Norbert.

I said, 'Yes, I'll have some coffee . . . black coffee.'

Leny left the room.

I'd already adjusted my watch to Berlin time. It was now 5.45 p.m. Through the window I saw the street lights were on, and the stars were out in the sky. I know for sure that the drug would show no effects till the next morning. Therefore, after my coffee I said to Norbert, 'I've heard of a famous road in Berlin—Kurfürstendamm. Can one see that?'

'Are you ready for a walk?' the lad asked me.

'Of course. At home I walk four miles a day.'

The walk left me with mixed feelings. Strange indeed! I thought. This is a police state led by an utterly corrupt leadership but you can't make it out from the citizens. The roads were quite crowded but peaceful. Malls or department stores were brightly lit up and well-dressed gatherings thronged the cinemas and theatres. When I mentioned this to Norbert, he said, 'That's precisely why when people visit this place for a brief spell, they begin to doubt what they have heard about Hitler's rule.'

In one clothing store in Kurfürstendamm, when I was checking out some pullovers, coats and trousers, I felt a soft push on my right elbow. Turning around, I saw a middle-aged woman staring at me.

'Professor Shonku?' the lady enquired with much hesitation. When I nodded my head, came the next question. '*Sprechen sie* deutsch?' Do you speak in German?

When I nodded my head once again, sheer joy reflected on that lady's face for a second before being replaced with a grief-stricken face. She held on to my hands and in a plaintive tone said, '*Helfen mich bitte, helfen mich*, Herr Professor!' Please, Professor, please help me. When asked what the matter with her was, she said she had been suffering from acute sinusitis and migraine for thirty years. 'You know, to date no one has invented any cure for a common cold. Please, please give me your *Allheilmittel* Miracurall pill!'

'Allheilmittel' means that which destroys all diseases. The lady had a terribly blocked nose and it was clear she was suffering.

'What's your name?' asked Norbert.

'Fraulein Fizenar', she said. Mrs Fizenar.

I said, 'I can give you one but under one condition. That you won't tell anyone.'

She nodded her head vigorously and promised she wouldn't tell anyone.

I was carrying four pills in my pocket, two of which I had powdered and given to Professor Steiner. I now gave the remaining two to Mrs Fizener.

'Do you have a piece of paper and pencil with you?' asked Norbert.

Saying 'Ja, ja', the lady took out a small notebook and pencil from her bag. Norbert put down his residence phone number in it and said, 'Call up any time tomorrow and let the professor know how you feel.'

The lady vanished into the crowd, thanking us profusely, repeating the words *Danke schoen, danke schoen*.

We decided to have dinner at a restaurant in Kurfürstendamm. I kept hoping no one else would recognize me.

When we returned home at 9 p.m. I went to the professor's bedroom and found him sleeping. I asked Leny, 'Has you father said anything during this time?'

Leny said, 'He mentioned my mother's name once more. And at one point, he said, "I'm coming."'

I sighed sadly and entered my room. Oh Lord, let Miracurall not fail.

They had allocated me a small but comfortable room. On the bedside table, I noticed a chocolate and card inscribed in a feminine writing. '*Gut Nacht*'. Good night. In her mother's absence, Leny had already become a mature homemaker.

Due to the hectic activities of the day, I slept soundly. In Giridih, I get up at 5 a.m. but when I woke up in the morning in Berlin, the clock in my room said it was five to six. Perhaps a feather pillow facilitates deep sleep.

I got out of bed. The moment my feet touched the floor a voice reached me—a rich melodious voice. But what did I hear? This was Sanskrit and the words were all too familiar to me! *Vedahametang purushangmahantamadityavarnang tamasah parastat . . .*

I'd heard my father recite this in my childhood, and I remember it well even today.

I put on a coat and walked towards the chanting.

The voice was coming from the professor's room.

Twameva viditwatimrityometi nanya pantha vidyate haynay.

The professor's room was empty. There was no one in bed. I noticed a door leading out to a balcony. With bated breath I went through and saw Professor Steiner standing on one side of the balcony, his back to me, facing the first light in the sky, reciting from the Upanishads.

Hearing my footsteps, he stopped midway, turned towards me, stared at me for a spell and, somewhat surprised, asked me, '*Kostvam?*' That is, in Sanskrit, who are you?

I replied in German. 'My name is Trilokeshwar Shonku.'

'Trilokeshwar? Vishnu, Shiva or Surya?'

I knew my name denotes all three. With a faint smile I said, 'None of these. I teach science in India. I've found an amazing Ayurvedic drug which works for all diseases. In London—'

'Miracurall?' the gentleman interrupted me. 'I've recovered after taking your medicine? That's why I was thinking . . . I have faced nothing but hard times in the last four years . . . why such compassion from God now? But, Trilokeshwar, I had accepted death; there's no point living any more!'

'But there is, Professor Steiner. Yesterday your son was saying that after you get well, he will somehow find a way for you to get away from Germany. Even if one needs to resort to any act of deception. You're familiar with the phrase *Shathe Shathyam* (tit for tat). In this nation, in such dark times, there is no point in thinking of rules. You settle anywhere abroad and start your work anew.'

This striking pandit said aloud to himself, 'Paris! André . . . André Varsova . . . my friend . . . he too is an Indologist . . . he has requested me to come over many a time . . . to come over . . .'

'Very well, that's where you'll go!'

Steiner had a glazed expression as the sun rose. 'So much work is left to be done! So much work to be completed! They never allowed me to do any work. What an irony of fate! The Nazi party—to merely utter this name poisons the mind—they are using the swastika as their symbol, emblem! *Su*, i.e., fine; *asti*, i.e., its presence; hence, *Swasti*, and from there we arrive at *Swastik*. They call it Swastika! Rather—'

The professor suddenly ceased his diatribe. I too became alert. There was a loud knocking at the main door. Not once, but three times.

'It's them, again,' said Steiner, sounding anxious.

Suddenly we saw Norbert and Leny rushing on to the balcony. They both gaped in awe at seeing their father standing up, looking normal.

Norbert was the first to recover. He dragged his father back into the room and told him to lie down. 'You need to pretend to be really sick, Papa,' he said. 'The Gestapo have arrived once more.'

The instant Steiner lay down, Leny pulled the quilt over him up to his chin and made him shut his eyes, with his mouth wide open.

'*Koekhe sie*, Papa!' she said, meaning he should start panting like an asthmatic patient.

Meanwhile, the knocking on the door downstairs had grown in volume. Norbert left the room. I followed him.

When we opened the door, the armed police marched straight inside the house. At once, their attention shifted from Norbert to me. Then they raised their right hands and said, 'Heil Hitler!'

Complete silence from me provoked them to raise their voice considerably.

'Heil Hitler!'

Sarvanashe samutpanne ardhang tyajati panditah.

Why just half, I abandoned all dignity and just to avoid any unpleasantness, raised my right hand, and in an impressive raucous voice uttered the words, 'Heil Hitler.' If Professor Steiner can act, why should I mind?

Later I realized, the German official was not Gestapo but Gestapo's minor relative, the 'Blackshirt'.

Blackshirt lowered his hand and said to me, 'Come along with me, quick. Schnell!'

What the hell was he saying? I asked, 'Where?'

'That you will get to know in due course. Put on some decent clothes and carry whatever you possess.'

I realized I was cornered; I would have to obey their instructions. I said, 'Give me five minutes. I'll go and get dressed.'

After changing my clothes, I noticed the Luger automatic given to me by Saunders in my suitcase. I knew they would search me, but I still put it inside my trouser pocket.

When I was about to leave the room, Norbert arrived, pale-faced, tears in his eyes.

'Please forgive me, Professor!'

I put my hand on his shoulder and said, 'Don't be silly. I don't think they will come back to torture your father again. You should discuss your escape plans. Don't worry about me at all. My intuition never lies and my mind tells me the time has not yet come for me to face death. You must carry on with your duties. You don't have much of a future in this country. Your father wants to go to Paris. Start organizing your departure and concentrate only on that. And always remember, under the present circumstances—faking, forging, fraudulence, taking refuge in lying—nothing's unfair.'

Norbert wiped his tears with a handkerchief and said, 'One last thing . . .'

'What's it?'

'Mrs Fizener called. She is cured of her sinusitis.'

Bidding goodbye to Norbert and Leny, I left with the police. There was a huge black car waiting for us. As I'd never seen this model before I couldn't help but ask its name. It was a Daimler.

I sat in the back seat, accompanied by Blackshirt. I had only one more question: 'May I please know where we're heading?'

'Carinhall,' was the reply.

All I could gather was that we were heading north. It was a big and comfortable car; the road was so smooth you could hardly feel you were in a vehicle. After fifteen minutes, I dozed off.

When I woke up, I found a complete change in the scenario. We had left the city and had arrived in a rural area.

The flora and fauna, farmland, small farmers' cottages—in all a serene surrounding so typical of a European countryside but has no resemblance to our Indian villages!

I was feeling a bit awkward and asked my escort: 'I'm sure you know my name; may I know yours?'

'Erich Fromm.'

The scenery outside changed further. Now the presence of trees had increased. Instead of open spaces, there were orchards on both sides of the road, though it being winter, all the trees had shed their leaves.

Soon the orchards on the left side of the road were replaced by a long wall. After driving for a while along the wall, we turned into a huge gate and drove for at least half a minute on a wide cobble-stoned driveway. Where had we arrived? Up till now I hadn't spotted any signs of habitation.

One last turn and we reached our destination. There was no doubt that this was a palace though not a very old one. It showed signs of renovation. A garden was spread out with well-laid flower beds, a lily pool, marble statues, and bounding the garden on three sides rested the palace. Our car stopped in front of one of its large main doors. We alighted from the car, passed by the guard, walked through the door to enter the palace.

We entered a huge hall that was at least fifty yards in length. I've never seen such a living example of opulence. Huge chandeliers hung overhead and the walls were decorated with gilt-framed oil paintings by world-famous painters. On the far side of the room, a spiral staircase rose to the first floor.

From here, we crossed over to another room which could be called a reception room. Apart from various sofa sets and fancy chairs, there was also a large table on the other side on which was kept papers and files, a telephone, a vase of flowers and a jug of water.

Erich Fromm gestured towards a sofa and he himself sat on a decorative chair kept in a corner.

After silently walking over a thick Persian carpet, I sat in a sofa that was so soft that I sank four inches. I was clueless about why I had been brought there. I did, however, notice that on seeing me enter the palace, one retainer had gone straight up to the first floor.

After five minutes of waiting, I was startled when all the clocks in the palace started chiming the hour. It was 8 o'clock. Erich Fromm suddenly leapt out of his chair to stand at attention and raised his right hand to say, 'Heil Hitler!' even as a pot-bellied man dressed in a double-breasted grey suit walked into the room.

He came towards me and said, '*Sprechen sie* deutsch?' He was asking me if I spoke German. I realized I'd seen his pictures. When I said 'Yes' he came a few steps closer to me and asked his second question.

'*Kennst du mich?*' Do you know me?

I said, 'The majority of those who read newspapers in India are familiar with your figure, Herr Göring.'

'I come right after Hitler in the hierarchy here,' Göring said, pacing up and down. 'I am the main force behind the German army. There's no country to match up with Germany in land, water or in the sky.'

I remained silent.

'Do you know where you've arrived?' he asked as he stopped walking and stood right in front of me.

I said, 'Carinhall.'

'Do you know what Carinhall is?'

'Perhaps your residence?'

'Carin was my first wife's name. Carin von Kantzow. She died in 1931. Before this, the Carinhall was a hunting lodge. After buying it, I turned it into a palace. It's an edifice in memory of Carin; and also my country house . . . all in one. In a not too distant future Carinhall will become one of the most noted mansions of this world.'

No more words were spoken. Yet I could strongly feel that Göring was looking at me fixedly.

Göring now voiced the question I was waiting for.

'What were you doing at number 17 Friedrichstrasse, the house of that barbaric Jew, Steiner?'

I needed to think before I opened my mouth. Should I spill out the truth or simply lie? Then it struck me that maybe by lying I could escape temporarily but it would take no time for their secret police to ferret out the real facts. Therefore, summoning up all my courage, I said,

'As Professor Steiner's life was under threat, due to police torture, I was brought over from London to treat him.'

'Miracurall worked?'

'It has.'

Göring's eyes gleamed.

'We want to eradicate this race, yet you're showing compassion to one of them? Do you know what Jews are?'

Before I could say anything, Göring used five adjectives about the Jews: *grausam; nieder; gierig; listig; bedenkenlos.* Barbaric; lowly; greedy; cunning; unscrupulous.

My contempt for this man was increasing and I became enraged when I heard his last few words. I said, 'I don't believe in any race. I'm a scientist. I worship one Jewish scientist like a God. His name is Albert Einstein.'

Göring's face turned red.

'Do you think Steiner will be spared?'

'Not thinking, but hoping.'

'I will crush all your hope under my feet. Steiner survives only for today. We won't let a single Jew flee. It's they who took our country towards a path of destruction. Just like a weed, each one needs to be uprooted individually.'

I had no stomach for this anti-Jew tirade. Adopting a somewhat harsh tone I said, 'Herr Göring, may I please know why I have been brought here?'

In a rather embarrassed tone, Göring said, 'We haven't brought you here without a reason. My intention was to show my country house to an Indian. I have never met any Indians before this. But that is not the real intent.'

'What then?'

Göring stared hard at me. 'What do you make of my health?'

I looked at him carefully. 'A stout man like you can't clearly be healthy, and I've never seen anyone sweat so much. In these ten minutes, you've taken out your handkerchief to wipe your face five times. Of course, since I'm not a doctor I don't know what exactly your ailment is.'

Turning hysterical, Göring suddenly raised his voice and said in a high-pitched voice: 'Do you know that due to this sweat I need to change my shirt eight times a day? Do you know that I weigh 170 kg? Do you know what *drüse* is?'

'I know.'

Drüse in English is a gland.

'This drüse is the root cause of all my trouble,' said Göring. 'My doctor knows this. Yet despite numerous treatments, nothing has helped me so far. It's not that I don't indulge in any physical work; I walk, I play tennis, though I need to instruct the person I play with that the ball must fall within my hand's range as I can't run. Apart from this, I hunt regularly. However—'

'What about food? Eating in excess is one prime reason for gaining weight.'

Göring said, 'I'm far too fond of food. Eating four times a day is not enough for me. I need to have sandwiches, beer and sausages every hour. I know of many other gluttons who are not obese like me, nor do they perspire so much. Do you know how much this excess fat hampers my work input?'

When he received no comment from me, Göring once more opened his mouth.

'What all diseases have you cured using your medicine?'

'Cancer, tuberculosis, dropsy, asthma, diabetes . . . '

'In that case your medicine will definitely cure my gland-related ailment. How many pills must a patient consume?'

'On an average two pills and to be taken only once.'

'How many days does it take to take effect?'

'In my experience it doesn't take more than twenty-four hours.'

'Do you have the medicine with you?'

'I was asked to carry all my belongings with me.'

'Then give two to me. I'll have them right now.'

'I'll give you the medicine, Herr Göring, but under one condition.'

'What's it?'

'Along with his son and daughter, Professor Steiner will leave for Paris tomorrow. You give the instructions in the right quarters that no one will stop them from leaving.'

Göring not only turned red in the face but also began to shake all over. Wiping away his sweat he roared, the room almost vibrating with his voice, 'You belong to a race which has been subjugated for over 200 years and yet you have this audacity! Erich, I want to search this man and his belongings. You aim a revolver at him.'

I'd almost forgotten about Erich Fromm's existence. Now he hurriedly came forward, took out his revolver from the waistband, aiming it at me. When Göring came towards me, I raised my hand.

'Halt, Herr Göring!'

Taken aback, he said, 'What do you mean?'

I'd already decided that what I'd say would work best under the present circumstances.

'I found this drug in my dream, Herr Göring,' I said in a controlled voice. 'I found the tree from which this drug is produced in my dream. I've also learnt that if this medicine is administered forcefully it'll not only yield no result, it may harm in fact. Would you like to change your shirt twelve times instead of eight? Would you like to weigh 200 kg instead of 170? It's pointless to aim a revolver at me, Herr Göring. Ask Erich to leave. I'll take out the medicine bottle from my bag, and you will remove all obstacles put in the way of Steiner's travel, and then I'll provide you with the medicine.'

It took a while for Göring to comprehend my words. Then he signalled Erich Fromm to put down his revolver, picked up the phone and said, 'Connect me to Anton.'

From what transpired on the phone, it was clear that instructions were given to this Anton to remove all obstacles in the way of Steiner's escape.

After putting down the phone, Göring took the flask kept on the table, poured water in a glass, took it in his hand and stood in front of me.

'Now give me your tablets. Not two, four.'

I opened my bag, took out four tablets from the bottle and placed these in Göring's hand. Göring gulped them down at one go.

I said, 'Now am I free to leave?'

'Not at all,' said Göring in his rumbling voice.

'What do you mean?'

'You won't earn your freedom with such ease. If in two days I see I'm no longer sweating, only then I'll be

convinced that your drug has worked. After two days, your pill will be chemically analysed. If—'

I interrupted him and said, 'It has already been analysed in London. The pill has one component that can't be identified. With the result—'

Göring cut me short and said, 'To hell with the British! Are you comparing a London laboratory with ours? We'll manufacture this pill artificially.'

'Then release it in the market?' I asked.

'No way! This drug will be used only by our party men. Those who are heading the party too are suffering from various ailments. Hitler's blood pressure shoots up after every speech. Goebbels had suffered from paralysis since childhood, which is why he walks with a limp. This is not very pleasant for a party spokesperson. He needs to walk straight. Himmler suffers from hysteria and endures migraine. Hence, till the laboratory report arrives you need to stay back. Well, have you had your breakfast?'

'No.'

'I'm going upstairs to change my shirt. I'm telling my fellow to give you breakfast.'

Göring left the room. I was shaking. Who knew that I would end up in the clutches of the Nazis? There's no way I could even inform Saunders about this. Also, I had no idea when I could return. What upset me the most was the thought that they might be able to identify the unknown in Miracurall and use my beloved Swarnaparnee to cure ailments of these wicked Nazi men.

I suddenly realized Erich was staring at me with a strange expression, as if trying to tell me something and summoning up his courage to do so.

After we exchanged glances, Erich got up from his chair and, looking somewhat humble, stood in front of me.

'What is it, Erich?'

'Herr Professor,' Erich said in an aggrieved tone, 'Since last month, an ailment has struck me due to which I may even lose my job.'

'What is it?'

'Epilepsy.'

Epilepsy is an awful disease. It can strike you suddenly. It can also lead to seizures and fainting.

'I have had fits thrice,' said Erich. 'I'm lucky I haven't had any attacks while I've been at work. I've consulted a doctor and I'm under medication. But it may take long to recover. I've lost my sleep with anxiety. Dear Professor, I've no one but you to turn to.'

To observe a Blackshirt in such a state made me both laugh as well as take pity on the man. The bottle was inside my pocket; I took out two pills and gave these to Erich.

'*Vier, bitte, vier!*' He too was asking for four!

I passed on two more. After gulping these down, he thanked me profusely and got back to his seat.

Göring had gone to change his shirt. How much time would that take? Ten minutes? I reclined on the sofa and pulled my left leg over the right, looking up at the plastered motifs on the ceiling and thinking of all that had taken place in the last twenty-four hours. What an amazing experience! Whatever one had read about Germany and the Nazis in the newspapers was all happening right in front of my eyes!

Realizing that I had some time on my hands, I took out my notebook from my suitcase and began to jot down my experiences in Berlin. I had begun writing my diary ever since I boarded the ship from Bombay.

After writing for a while, I had to stop because I was disturbed by a strange sound.

I turned to look at Erich Fromm. His head had bent forward to his chest. The sound I had heard was of him snoring. Well! Well! Such a duty-bound ever-alert officer! He had fallen asleep while watching over me! If Göring turned up now, what a to-do there would be!

But where was Göring? I wondered if four pills had been an overdose and taking extra pills induces deep sleep. That I've been giving only two so far was on the basis of a conjecture on my part: as the first case was cured by two pills, I felt that was the correct dose to give.

I wrote in my diary for another five minutes and then got up. The sound of Erich's snoring had increased manifold and sounded like a jackhammer. As Göring also was showing no sign of coming down, I was convinced that he too had fallen asleep.

Silently, I emerged from the room and stepped into the big hall. I saw a servant carrying a breakfast tray approaching me. Seeing me outside the room took him by surprise and he said, '*Ihre frühstück*, Herr Professor.' Frühstück is breakfast.

I said, 'So I can see, but can you tell me why my boss is taking so long?'

'Ja, ja.'

'Why?'

'*Herr schlafen.*' That is, he is sleeping. Which means my guess was right.

I asked the servant to keep the breakfast on the table and he went inside the reception room.

A sheer stroke of luck this was. I had to encash it. I ran out of the hall and left the palace. When I reached the driveway, I saw the Daimler parked there. The driver was strolling around the car, his hands inside his pockets.

I went forward. I had decided what I would do.

Seeing me, the driver straightened up in surprise. His hands came out from his pockets.

I went up to him and said, 'Take me to Berlin. Drop me where you'd picked me up from.'

The driver gesticulated to protest.

'*Nein, nein, das kann ich nicht.*' No, I cannot do that.

I raised my hand and showed him the Luger Saunders had given me. 'Now you can?'

The driver's face turned pale. 'Ja, ja ja.' He himself opened the door for me. Within half an hour, I reached the Steiner residence.

All three in the Steiner family shot up from their chairs when they saw me. Professor Steiner gave me a warm hug. Norbert said, 'What happened? Where did they take you?'

I narrated everything briefly and said, 'Start preparing for your departure right away. You leave for Paris by tomorrow. No one will stop you from leaving. I'll return to London by this evening's flight. Norbert, please help me with my booking.'

Sitting in the 4 o'clock flight, I realized I was fighting two differing conflicts within my mind. Just as I got immense joy at being able to save at least one Jewish family from the Nazis, I was revolted by the idea that my medicine was curing two abominable demons of their illness.

Saunders never thought I would return that early. Everyone was eager to find out what had transpired in Berlin. 'First let us know if your trip was a success.'

I said, 'At one level it was a remarkable success. Steiner is cured and all their crises are now solved.'

'Bravo!'

'But if I club with this with another matter, it will not amuse you.'

'What's that?'

'You were right, Saunders.'

'You fell into a Nazi trap?'

'Yes.'

I described the Blackshirt–Göring–related incident breathlessly and said, 'There would have been no problem if four of my Miracurall pills had only put them to sleep in order to help me escape but that my medicine has cured two dreadful fiends makes me feel awful. Believe me, Saunders, when I say that I feel terrible!'

But wait! Why did I see a faint smile on Saunders's lips?

He now put his hand inside his pocket and took out an unfamiliar bottle containing white pills.

'Here, take your Miracurall.'

'What do you mean?'

'Very simple. That day Dorothy and you left for a walk and I stayed back to write my article, I opened your bag, took out the Miracurall pills from your bottle and replaced them with the sure, hit sleeping pill, Seconal. Four Seconal pills at one go is a deadly affair . . . assured sleep inevitable within ten minutes! My dear Shonku, I didn't want your precious medicine to fall into the hands of the world's lowest of low creatures. I didn't! I didn't! I didn't!'

All dark thoughts left my mind. I held Saunders's hand in mine in great relief.

Translator's Note

Year 1961: Centenary of Rabindranath Tagore; construction of the Berlin Wall; flight of the first human, Soviet astronaut Yuri Gagarin, into space . . . Yes, these are all significant milestones that marked the year but what served as a moment of lollapalooza for me was coming across the annual issue of *Sandesh* magazine that appeared in October 1961.

What emerged from it was the first instalment of a whimsical story, 'The Diary of a Space Traveller', featuring an equally whimsical scientist named Professor Trilokeshwar Shonku. At the age of fifty, Professor Shonku builds a rocket (using toadstools, snakeskins and the empty shells of tortoise eggs along with aqueous vellosilica) and, from the backyards of his house in Giridih, hoots off to Mars along with his robot Bidhushekhar, retainer Prahlad and the twenty-four-year-old cat, Newton. After some mishaps in Mars, the rocket lands on the planet Tafa.

This extraordinary adventure marked the first-ever appearance of science fiction (or fantasy?) for children in Bengal, perhaps also in India. Who knew that Professor

Shonku's one-way ticket to an unknown planet, Tafa, would lead to such years of sheer joy amongst many generations of readers? All thanks to a chance finding of his first diary (subsequently, twenty-one more were found in his laboratory) resting on a crater of a meteorite, containing thirty-eight full-fledged adventures and the beginning of two new adventures. An additional delight was to read each escapade written in the form of a diary. I don't know how many children of today's generation actually understand the charm of maintaining and browsing through a diary.

Professor Shonku is a single, simple, solitary man, tucked away in a house in Giridih. His escapades begin from his homeland and go beyond Bengal to stretch across the world. Further, he travels not just by land, air and water, but even through time, through continents like Europe, Africa, South America, ancient civilizations, deserted terrains, unknown islands, even going underwater in the sea in Gopalpur and back to the compound of his house and the cremation ground of Giridih. The range and variety of these locations perfectly match the diversity of his adventures. Though a loner by nature, his life revolves around an intimate group: a trusting man Friday, Prahlad; his feline friend, Newton; his sceptical neighbour, Abinash Babu; Bengal-based clairvoyant and sincere well-wisher, Nakur Chandra Biswas; British geologist, Jeremy Saunders; German anthropologist, Wilhelm Crole, and the English scientist, John Summerville.

More an inventor rather than a hardcore scientist, Shonku is inclined to put together scientific gadgets with commodities found within his immediate neighbourhood, always using local flora and fauna, herbs, extracts from the roots of trees, ash from a funeral pyre, rainwater and the like. Certainly in today's parlance everything he used was strictly organic! In his lifetime he invented well over sixty instruments beginning with a snuff gun, Nasyastra, which caused a person to sneeze fifty-six times non-stop, and eventually to numerous other more complicated devices which remain a subject of envy in the scientific fraternity even today.

Though originating on a note of the absurd and whimsy, some of his inventions ring so true *now*, for instance, the half-a-pea-sized blue pebble that contains the solution to the human race's four major crises along with its 65,000 years of history. Isn't the entire world now very familiar with this concept of miniaturization? Or for that matter a computer turning aggressive and outsmarting you?

Very unlike a cut-and-dried scientist, Shonku, in his exposure to a gamut of experiences, has always addressed grey areas with great cogency. For a long time he firmly believed that one day subjects such as ghosts and spectres, séances, telepathy and clairvoyance will become subjects of scientific studies. Many readers familiar with Shonku narratives can easily connect plots that address these issues.

One major highlight of Shonku's adventures is that in them young readers can learn a great deal about world affairs—history, culture, geography, personalities, discoveries and, above all, oddities of human behaviour. Lessons are imparted obliquely to show what malice, greed, jealousy, insecurity can do to a man. Ray gently steers the actions from wrong to right while not once deviating from the main plot. Another facet that always appealed to my young mind as a reader was Shonku's deep empathy with all living beings—the bird and the animal kingdom in particular. Time and again, he dealt with important characters of birds like macaw, crow, animals like gorillas, slow loris, dogs, cats and even his invention of a magnificent being, EA. With each such creature, he highlighted their sparkling intelligence, emotions, ethos and their ability for quick comprehension to combat tricky situations and dissect any foul play and at the right time display the capacity to expose the culprit.

In this last volume of Professor Shonku's exploits, this multilingual brilliant and benevolent scientist typically travels around the world once more to face near-death situations. Each nerve-wracking experience is faithfully recorded in his diary. We learn of Shonku being outwitted by his own invention, the Tellus computer; his helplessness when his arch-rival in Rome deliberately misplaces his wonder drug, Miracurall; how another drug invented by Shonku, Alixirum, plays a vital role in unravelling the identity of a primitive being; and the thrilling discovery of a *3500-year-old* sparkling diamond necklace as well as a papyrus in an ancient tomb in Cairo. We also accompany the ever-adventurous Shonku on a trip to the past in a time machine; and on a journey to Ingolstadt to study Victor Frankenstein's formula to rejuvenate the dead; and how the discovery of a drug similar to the drug in Robert Louis Stevenson's *Dr Jekyll and Mr Hyde* leads Shonku and an Italian scientist through an exhilarating adventure.

A pronounced subterranean theme running through many of the nine stories in this volume is that of Nazism. The last story of this volume has Shonku in a reminiscing and ruminative mood, contemplating the events of his past, the teachings of his father, his formative years, his numerous discoveries, and finally to a crucial encounter with none other than the horrifying Hermann Göring. This adventure perhaps epitomizes the merging of the persona of Ray and Shonku into one seamless character.

A special attraction of this volume is the story 'Tellus', translated by the author himself. It first appeared in *The Stories* (1987). It's interesting to note that the first translation of Ray's fiction was neither of his short stories nor of his ever-popular mystery stories featuring Feluda, the sleuth. They were a short selection of Shonku stories, *Bravo! Professor Shonku*, translated by Kathleen M. O'Connell in 1983 and published by Rupa. In 1987, Ray himself did a few more for Secker and Warburg (*Stories*) and in 1994 appeared *The Incredible Adventures of Professor Shonku*, translated by Surabhi Banerjee, published by Penguin India. And then came the freshly translated volumes of Shonku adventures published by Puffin Books in 2004: *The Diary of a Space Traveller and Other Stories* followed by *The Unicorn Expedition and Other Stories* translated by Gopa Majumdar. In 2015, Puffin published the third volume, *The Mystery of Munroe Island and Other Stories*. There are two incomplete stories that have been omitted from this anthology as they were essentially in a preliminary and unfinished state. But barring those, the entire Shonku adventures are now available in Puffin.

Last but not the least, in 2019, as we all know, Shonku, for the first time, travelled to yet another hitherto-unknown land—the silver screen—appearing in a bilingual film (Bengali and English) directed by Sandip Ray, *Professor Shanku O El Dorado*. Needless to add, Shonku in his new avatar was an immediate success among his young viewers. As a translator my concern is: Will children forget to meet Shonku within printed pages and only reach out for his screen image? Will they no longer play out his adventures in their own fantasy? No! Nyet! Nein! Ray's magic with words (in the original Bengali as well as in English translation) will hopefully keep alive the genius of Prof. Trilokeshwar Shonku within the world of papyrus!

Indrani Majumdar
April 2020

Indrani Majumdar lives in Delhi but has her roots firmly based in Bengali culture. Her bilingualism has helped her career as she has translated Bengali texts into English and vice versa. A keen researcher, her vocation in life has been to explore the various facets of Satyajit Ray's work. At present she works with the Programme Office, India International Centre, Delhi.

Acknowledgements

My thanks go to Penguin India for producing this final
volume and, in particular, to Sohini Mitra for asking me
to translate these; and to Sandip Ray for allowing us to use
Ray's original drawings for this volume. I sincerely hope
the present generation of readers will pick up this volume
and travel with Shonku on his escapades across the globe.

Copyright Acknowledgements

Many of Satyajit Ray's stories were first published in the annual Durga Puja magazine, *Sharodiya*. The following are the dates of publication of the stories.

1. Tellus (First published in *Anandamela* 1978)
2. Professor Rondi's Time Machine (First published in *Anandamela* 1985)
3. Nefrudet's Tomb (First published in *Sandesh* 1986)
4. Shonku and the Primordial Man (First published in *Anandamela* 1986)
5. Shonku's Date with History (First published in *Anandamela* 1987)
6. Shonku and Frankenstein (First published in *Anandamela* 1988)
7. Dr Danielli's Discovery (First published in *Sandesh* 1988)

Published by Corgi Children's Books, published in
Australia, 1992

The Tea with Grandma Jesse Class, first published in
Australia, 1990

CONTENTS

AUTHOR FILE

NAME: Satyajit Ray

BORN: 2 May 1921, in a progressive Brahmo family of Kolkata

FATHER: Sukumar Ray, famous writer, poet and printing technologist

MOTHER: Suprabha Ray

QUALIFICATIONS: BA in Economics (Hons) from Presidency College, Kolkata. Trained in Oriental Arts for three years at Visva-Bharati University

PROFESSIONAL LIFE: Worked in the advertising agency DJ Keymer for almost twelve years. Started as a junior visualizer and went on to become the art director

MARRIED TO: Bijoya Ray

CHILDREN: One son, Sandip Ray, also a film-maker

FAMOUS FOR: Internationally acclaimed films. One of the earliest Indian directors to have won prizes at major film festivals around the world like Cannes, Venice, Berlin, London and San Francisco. An extremely versatile person, he wrote the script, composed the music, designed the sets and costumes, prepared posters in addition to directing the films. Ray was also a writer of repute, and his short stories, novellas, poems and articles, written in Bengali, are still immensely popular. Many of his books became bestsellers. He also illustrated them.

MAJOR AWARDS: Bharat Ratna, highest civilian award of India; Legion D'Honneur, highest civilian award of France; and the Oscar for Lifetime Achievement

SHONKU FACT FILE

FULL NAME: Trilokeshwar Shonku. In Bengali, Shonku means a cone. Trilokeshwar means the 'lord of heaven, earth and hell'. It is also a play on the name Trishanku, a mythical figure who tried to reach the heavens but was punished by the gods to forever remain stranded somewhere between heaven and earth.

BIRTHDAY: 16 June. Birth year estimated to be 1912

QUALIFICATIONS: BSc in physics and chemistry. A child prodigy, he graduated from college when he was sixteen. Honorary doctorate from the Swedish Academy of Sciences

HOMETOWN: Giridih

PET: Cat called Newton

MANSERVANT: Prahlad

NEIGHBOUR: Avinash Babu

FRIENDS: William Crole Jeremy Saunders, John Summerville

How did Professor Shonku come to be?
The first book in which Prof. Shonku appeared was simply called Professor Shonku. Published in 1965, it was Ray's first book, though the stories had been written between 1961 and 1965. Professor Shonku was dedicated to Ray's son, Sandip, who was eleven years old then. The inscription in the original book read 'To Sandip Babu'. (Sandip's pet name is Babu.) This was

the only time Ray dedicated any of his books. One of the earliest examples of science-fiction writing in any Indian language, this book won the Government of India's prize for Best Book for the Young.

POLITICS, PERSONALITIES AND HISTORY

Second World War

The Second World War was the deadliest war in all of human history with around 70 million people killed. It involved two groups of countries, the 'Allies' and the 'Axis'. The major Allied Powers were Britain, France, Russia, China and the United States. The major Axis Powers were Germany, Italy and Japan. Among the allies were the entire British Empire including United India, Burma, many African countries including South Africa, Australia, New Zealand and Canada.

Before the Second World War began, Germany was ruled by a man named Adolf Hitler who came to power in 1933.

Together with the Nazi Party, he wanted Germany to rule Europe. On 1 September 1939, German troops invaded Poland. Soon, Britain and France declared war on Germany—the Second World War had begun.

By the summer of 1941, German forces had invaded France, Belgium, Holland, Luxembourg, Denmark, Norway, Greece, Yugoslavia and then attacked USSR on 22 June 1941.

Hitler wanted to create what he thought was the 'best' and strongest race—and to the Nazi Party, this excluded certain groups, such as Jews, gypsies and those with physical and mental disabilities. Millions of Germans were imprisoned and killed because they didn't fit the image of the 'perfect' German. In an attempt to eliminate a 'racial enemy' outside of Germany, such groups were also persecuted in the countries invaded by German forces.

The group most heavily targeted by the Nazis were the Jews.

Around six million Jewish people were killed during the Second World War in one of history's most terrible events—the Holocaust. Racist in his views, Hitler blamed the Jewish people for Germany losing the First World War and claimed they were dangerous to German people and society. Hitler intensely hated the Slavic population which included Poles, Russians and the entire East Europe. His repulsion towards the black African was so acute that he refused to shake hands with Jesse Owens, the Olympian champion in sprinting at Berlin in 1936, even though he was an African-American.

Around the same time that Germany fought for power in Europe, Japan wanted to control Asia and the Pacific.

In 1937, under Emperor Hirohito, Japan attacked China, bringing the two nations into years of conflict.

The US didn't join the war until 1941, when Japan attacked the United States—at their Naval Base at Pearl Harbor in Hawaii. On 8 December 1941—the very next day—the US declared War on Japan and, in turn, its German allies.

Some countries remained 'neutral' in the Second World War. Such countries—Spain, Sweden, Switzerland, Portugal, Ireland and Turkey—chose not to join either side.

The Germans surrendered on 8 May 1945.

In 1944, an Allied army crossed from Britain to free France from Nazi rule. One year later, Allied armies invaded Germany, forcing the Germans to surrender. After nuclear attacks on Japan's major cities Hiroshima and Nagasaki, Japan also surrendered to Allied forces in August the same year. The Second World War had ended.

Among Hitler's closest associates were Joseph Goebbels (1897–1945), Heinrich Himmler (1900–45), Hermann Göring (1893–1946), Reinhard Heydrich (1904–42), Joachim von Ribbentrop (1893–1946), Bormann (1900–45) and others. After the war, a majority of them either committed suicide or were hanged after the Nuremburg trials, held in 1946.

The Tree with the Golden Leaves: This is the final entry received from the diaries of Professor Shonku before he went missing. The story is a classic example of Satyajit Ray weaving in facts to inform his readers about the world around them. Here he deals with Nazi Germany and Europe on the brink of the Second World War. We learn about:

Gestapo: The gestapo was the official secret police of Nazi Germany. It stands for Geheime Staatspolizei, 'secret state police'.

Blackshirt: Member of any of the armed squads of Italian fascists under Benito Mussolini, who wore black shirts as part of their uniform.

Time Machine

Travelling back into the past or forwards into the future is the stuff of science fiction and always has been.
  The Time Machine is a science fiction novella by H.G. Wells, published in 1895. The work is credited with the popularization of the concept of time travel by using a vehicle or device to travel purposely and selectively forwards or backwards through time. The term 'time machine', coined by Wells, is now almost universally used to refer to such a vehicle or device.
  One of the greatest and most famous physicists, Stephen Hawking, who is a master on the subject, believes that it's almost impossible to travel back in time.

Papyrus

Papyrus or *Cyperus papyrus* is a kind of paper that was used in Ancient Egypt for writing but were later used throughout the Mediterranean region. It grew about 10 foot high! It was first made as far back as the third millennium BC. The plant had a variety of uses. The Egyptians also used papyrus plants to make boats, mattresses, mats, rope, sandals and baskets. To make sure what they wrote down was protected, the ancient Egyptians only wrote on one side of a sheet (thin strip) of paper. When the paper was full of writing, they rolled the paper into a cylinder with the writing inside, and left a hole down the middle. That way, if the paper picked up any moisture, it could dry more easily.

INNOVATIONAL IDIOSYNCRASIES

Professor Shonku's inventions have set extremely high standards for scientists all across the world. Here is a list of some of his major inventions that will leave you awestruck and convinced of our beloved professor's incomparable genius:

Innovation	Description
Bidhushekhar	A rather comic robot, capable of inexplicably brilliant stuff
Mangorange	A hybrid fruit of mango and orange—tastes a bit of both
Invisibility Potion	A liquid version of Harry Potter's Invisibility Cloak!
Microsonograph	Device to record every tiny sound made in the world
Air-conditioning pill	A pill to keep in your pocket, which keeps you comfortable irrespective of the temperature
Electric pistol	Pistol to deliver an electric shock of 400 volts
Somnolin	Super-effective sleeping pill
Neospectroscope	Device to summon ghosts of the departed
Miracurall	Pill to miraculously cure all diseases
Room freshener	Natural fragrances of thirty-six flowers

Innovation	Description
Onmiscope	Telescope + Microscope + X-ray in a device that looks like a pair of normal spectacles
Ornithon	Device to impart knowledge to birds
Annihilin gun	A gun to make anything disappear
Remembrain	A helmet that helps you remember old or forgotten memories
Cerebrilliant	Nerve-soothing pill that helps recover quickly from head injuries
Shankalan	Extremely strong yet light plastic

Read More in Puffin Classics

The Diary of a Space Traveller and Other Stories
Satyajit Ray

It all began with the fall of a meteorite and the crater it made. In its centre was a red notebook, sticking out of the ground— the first (or was it really the last?) of Professor Shonku's diaries. Professor Trilokeshwar Shonku, eccentric genius and scientist, disappeared without a trace after he shot off into space in a rocket from his backyard in Giridih, accompanied by his loyal but not-too-intelligent servant, Prahlad, his cat, Newton, and Bidhushekhar, his robot with an attitude.

What has become of the professor? Has he decided to stay on in Mars, his original destination? Or has he found his way to some other planet and living there with strange companions? His last diary tells an incredible story . . . Other diaries unearthed from his abandoned laboratory reveal stranger and even more exciting adventures involving a ferocious sadhu, a revengeful mummy and a mad scientist in Norway who turns famous men into six-inch statues.

Exciting, imaginative and funny, the stories in this collection capture the sheer magic of Ray's lucid language, elegant style, graphic descriptions and absurd humour. The indomitable Professor Shonku has returned, to win himself over a whole new band of followers!

Read More in Puffin Classics

The Mystery of Munroe Island and Other Stories

Satyajit Ray

Join Professor Trilokeshwar Shonku, eccentric genius and scientist, on an incredible world tour as he confronts a daring doppelganger, undertakes an experiment to create pure gold, unravels the mystery of a scientist's loss of memory and visits an unknown island to look for an amazing fruit, amongst other escapades. What is the message in the mysterious papyrus found in Cairo and why did scientists go missing in the deep jungle of Congo? Is there any truth about the sightings of the UFO and what happens when he takes an extraordinary animal to Koblenz in Germany? Featuring the indomitable Professor Shonku and a bunch of madcap characters is presented here in a brilliant new translation that brings alive the magic and charm of Satyajit Ray's imaginative world. Get ready for some hair-raising fun with the weird and wonderful Prof. Shonku, whose exploits have held readers spellbound for over five decades.